CW00741487

THE SNOW VULTURE

by the same author

poetry

A DREAM OF MAPS (Raven Arts Press)
A ROUND HOUSE (Allison and Busby)
THE LAME WALTZER (Allison and Busby)
BLUE SHOES (Secker and Warburg)
CACTI (Secker and Warburg)

poetry for children

THE FLYING SPRING ONION

fiction for children

THE CHINESE DRESSING-GOWN (Raven Arts Press)

MATTHEW SWEENEY

The Snow Vulture

faber and faber
LONDON · BOSTON

First published in 1992
by Faber and Faber Limited
3 Queen Square London WC1N 3AU

Photoset by Parker Typesetting Service, Leicester
Printed in Great Britain by Clays Ltd, St Ives plc

A CIP record of this book is available from the British Library

ISBN 0–571–16603–2

2 4 6 8 10 9 7 5 3 1

For Malvin and Nico

The purple curtains were opened, showing a white, snow curtain on the outside of the window.

'Clive, Carl, wake up! Come and see the snow!'

At that moment the boys' alarm went off like a tin maniac, and kept going till it ran out. Clive sat on the edge of the bottom bunk, rubbing his eyes, before shambling over to the window. His mother tapped the panes with her finger and all the snow fell off, except for the thick snowy insulation on the wooden frame. Down below, the row of bins and all their spilt litter were clean. The trees had white leaves to replace the green. The parked ambulance and black taxi and red car had the same colour of roof. People were lifting their feet high as they walked, and losing them again in snow.

Carl was still in the top bunk, still under cover. His mother shook him and, reluctantly, his head came out, hair sticking up like a punk's. He took one look at the window and lay back again.

'Don't you see the snow?' Clive asked.

'So, who cares?' said Carl.

'I do. I love snow,' Clive said.

'Good for you.'

'Get dressed, both of you. And stop bickering.'

Clive was already out of the room before Carl dropped to the floor. When, a few minutes later, he too went upstairs to swallow breakfast, a stranger would have sworn he was seeing double. And it was true, the boys were the same height, had the same blond hair, same nose, mouth, chin. But no twins are ever alike to those who know them. In Clive's and Carl's case you could tell the difference from their eyes – in Clive's was calm, in Carl's badness. Even a stranger might have noticed.

It's rare enough to find twins who were born on different dates. It's extremely rare to find twins who were born in different years. Clive and Carl were born in different decades – Clive in the last minutes of 1979, Carl early in 1980, while the church bells and the strains of 'Auld Lang Syne' went on in the background. When Clive came out, the doctor and midwife thought that was it. But Carl followed. It might have been better the other way around.

On this February morning in 1991, however, such thoughts were irrelevant. The snow was on everyone's mind. The twins' mother was thinking about chains for the wheels of her car. Their father was talking about his childhood in the Black Forest in Germany, where they changed to special snow-tyres, and knew how to cope with – and enjoy – snow. Clive was thinking about how he'd enjoy it here in London easily enough. Even Carl was thinking this, though he pretended not to.

*

Clive stood at the bus-stop, hooded like a sentry in Siberia. He slapped his gloved hands against his sides in an effort to keep his fingers warm. All the while, he was being bombarded by snowballs. Carl had started this, but the other boys at the bus-stop weren't slow in joining in. Clive waited, without responding, until they got bored and turned on each other. Then, with his back to them, he made a big, firm snowball which he tossed from hand to hand like a freshly baked potato until the bus rounded the corner. Just as the door opened and people got off he hurled his snowball at Carl, hitting him full in the face.

He knew this would mean trouble, but if he did nothing he'd be pestered by Carl anyway. What a brother to have! If it wasn't snow it was something else, so he couldn't let him get away with everything. But retribution for his snowball strike was quicker than he'd anticipated. It came in the cold, wet form of snow sliding down the back of his shirt while his hands were pinned to his sides. And the whole bus watched this without stopping it.

At least the rest of the journey was peaceful – apart from Clive's fears that he'd get pneumonia from the snow now melted inside his shirt. On the way, they passed stationary cars with their drivers inside, and the engines going wurr-wurr-wurr, while husbands or wives threw boiling water on the windscreens. The twins' father was right. This country wasn't prepared for snow, just as it wasn't prepared for very hot summers. Both situations did happen occasionally, Clive thought. You'd think, in this age of refrigeration and air-conditioning, that the country would learn.

He had to suffer a few more snowballs when they got to school, including one in the classroom. The teacher kept the twins well separated – Clive had a seat by a radiator and a window, while Carl sat against the opposite wall. In between were three groups of tables. Sometimes, on very cold days, Carl tried to take Clive's seat, but he never got away with it. Even if Clive had been soft enough to let him, the teacher and the rest of the class wouldn't take long to spot the difference.

Even if they were truly indistinguishable, there would be no confusing their actions. Today was no exception. At break-time the boys in the class were asked to clear away snow from the steps and the path to the gate. They set to it, whooping – all except two, who were later spied up on the flat roof over the main entrance. One of them was one of the twins, and Clive wasn't the only one looking up who knew which twin it was. Though some day soon, he swore, he'd make himself do a Carl-type deed just to fool them.

Carl and his mate were busy gathering all the snow on the roof into a great big ball. Carl never had any problems getting accomplices in his mildly criminal activities. His popularity sickened Clive, who had friends too, but few in comparison with Carl. And neither set of friends liked the other. In fact, Carl's friends tended to bully Clive's. Clive himself escaped the worst of the bullying only because he was Carl's brother.

The snowball was now boulder-sized, and was being rolled around on the roof until it was tightly packed. Carl took a ruler and a roll of twine from his pockets, and he and the other boy somehow propped the huge snowball up on the ruler which was wedged in the drainpipe, leaving a third of the snowball hanging over the doorway. The twine had been tied to the ruler, of course, and was long enough to hang down on the far side of the entrance, in the shadow of a great elm, where it wouldn't be seen.

Clive waited with a mixture of irritation and grudging admiration as the two villains dropped to the snowy ground and took up their positions, Carl with the twine in his twitching fingers, his mate standing with his hands in his pockets among a group of fans right in front of the entrance. As soon as the Headteacher – a bald, plump Welshman – came to the door to ring the bell, Carl's mate began to whistle a tune from the top ten, and immediately the twine was pulled, the ruler jumped out, and the snow-boulder fell straight onto the Headteacher, burying him, until many small hands dug him out.

And even though they were kept in for three hours writing lines (it would have been worse if the Head wasn't such a jovial fellow), no one squealed on the culprits, and few minded the unearned punishment. They seemed to like Carl's nerve and the variety of his antics. Clive minded very much. He spent long enough in school as it was. He especially minded today, because he couldn't wait to build a snowman on the roof-garden. Now by the time they got home and had eaten and done their homework it would be bedtime.

*

It was Saturday. Normally both twins were out of bed at the streaks of dawn to watch kids' programmes on television. It was the one day Carl had no problem getting up. This morning, however, the television was cold and silent, and noises were coming down the stairs from the roof.

The twins had got over their squabble, and were busily scraping snow into two piles – Clive with a dustpan, Carl with a tin wastepaper bin. As it was only a small roof-garden, it would have been better for them to work together on one pile. The problem was that Carl didn't want to build a snowman.

'It's boring,' he said. 'That's what you always do.'

'It's not. How often do you get snow?' asked Clive.

'That's not the point. I want to build something different.'

'Like what?' taunted Clive. 'A snow-hill?'

'A snow vulture,' said Carl.

'Ugh, vultures. I hate them.'

'They're my favourite birds,' Carl almost shouted.

So they each decided to build what they wanted.

It didn't take them too long to leave the tiles bare, and all the snow in the two piles. Some snow still lay on the plants, but they'd been damaged enough, and any further poking would get the twins barred from the roof-garden. Carl's pile was bigger than Clive's, because a wastepaper bin is bigger than a dustpan, and this was especially unfair, as a man is bigger than a vulture. Carl looked at his pile and shook his head. For a minute he looked at Clive's, but he knew better than to start anything there.

'We need more,' he said.

'Maybe more snow will fall today,' said Clive.

'Maybe it'll melt,' Carl said. 'We can't wait.'

He thought for a while, then brightened up. 'I have an idea. Come with me.'

To get in from the roof-garden they had to rap on the glass door which their mum had shut to keep the cold from coming down the stairs. (There was no way of opening the door from the outside.) It was as well she hadn't forgotten, and gone shopping, as there wouldn't have been a lot they could have done. They couldn't even have smashed the glass and climbed through, as it was reinforced with graphpaper wire. But she came and let them in.

After a quick blast of heat on wet gloves and numb fingers, Carl led the way down to the communal back garden. It seemed wrong to call it a garden, as all it had were some ill-kept shrub-beds, a few skeletal trees, and a hedge interwoven with a wire railing. The rest was cement, including the bays for the black plastic rubbish bins, each with a name scrawled in white paint. But today it was a snow garden, with more than enough snow to build a snow hippopotamus, if they'd wanted.

They each piled some snow onto a bin lid (Carl borrowed a neighbour's) and, like masons carrying wet cement on hods, they laboured with them up the stairs, up five flights to the roof-garden. It was tough work, made even tougher by the tongue-thrashing their mum gave them for bringing snow through the flat. Their dad just looked at them and shrugged.

Carl was nothing if not stubborn, however. And inventive, when it suited him. His new idea was to rig up a crude pulley system with a rope and a plastic bucket. At first they tried to do it simply with the rope and a blanket thrown over the roof wall. Then, thinking of the wheels the ropes run on at building sites, they dug out a couple of paint rollers and wedged them in the bricks used for holding the barbecue. It wasn't brilliant, but it was better. They hauled up twenty or so buckets, taking turns to pull and to fill, and then they called it a day.

Building was easy after that. Perhaps a better word would be snow sculpture, such was the care both boys took, each trying to outdo the other. Admittedly, there is only so much that can be done with a snowman – the big head on the bulky, armless, legless body – but Clive made it as elegant as it was possible for a snowman to be. He painted eyes on eggshells and coaxed them into place – it took a few attempts as they cracked very easily. A downward-curving courgette was the nose, and for the mouth he chose a red plastic ring which he buried in the head so that only a few inches of the rim were showing. Even so, his snowman was far outclassed by Carl's snow vulture. It sat there, tall, gaunt, hunched and sinister, looking much more lifelike than Clive's man. It was all snow, except for two small lumps of smokeless coal for eyes. It was already the snow-boss of the roof-garden.

*

The twins stood in the entrance to the roof-garden. Carl had a snigger on his face, Clive was annoyed. His snowman had lost an eye and the nose, and it had only been there one day. Could it be thawing so quickly? It didn't feel any warmer and, besides, Carl's vulture was disgustingly in one piece.

Clive marched over and picked up the eggshell and the courgette from the snow and stuck them carefully back in place. The eggshell was cracked but he wasn't going to paint up another one. All the time he was aware of the black stare of the vulture. How come its eyes didn't fall out? Coal is heavier than eggshells. Unless it was the vulture who'd poked out the snowman's eyes and nose?

He threw that silly idea out of his mind at once, but glowered at the still-smirking Carl anyway. Maybe Carl himself had come upstairs in the night and maimed Clive's snowman. It would be just like him, except that by his standards the snowman had got off lightly. Clive gave him the benefit of the doubt and put it down to the thaw, wishing at the same time more snow would fall.

Carl was on his hunkers beside his vulture. He was making something else in snow, something small. Clive went over to investigate. It was a crude human figure, lying flat, with its arms and legs out, at the foot of the vulture. Carl saw Clive's interest.

'Do you like this dead body? It fell on its face from an aeroplane and I'm feeding my vulture with it.'

'You're disgusting,' Clive said.

'At least I feed my creatures,' Carl replied. 'Your snowman is breaking up from hunger.'

His harsh laughter followed Clive down the stairs and was only drowned out when Clive put the radio on loud. He stood with his bum to the fire until he thought he would smell roast meat, then he turned and did the same to the other side. Snow would be even better if it weren't so cold, but he knew that that was a contradiction, and, besides, he could put up with it. A lot easier than he could put up with his brother usually. There was no fire that could put right the effects of *him*.

*

Throughout that Sunday, Clive visited the roof-garden from time to time, like a policeman checking out the home of a threatened person. Happily the snowman was intact, and there was no feeling of thaw in the air. On the contrary, around 4 p.m., just as it was beginning to get dark, more snow began to drift down. Carl had spent most of the day on the roof-garden. Clive didn't know what his brother was up to, and didn't care, as long as his snowman was left alone. It had become very important to him that the snowman should hold its own up there. At bedtime it was still in good shape so Clive went to bed happy. Apart, that was, from the mischievous look in Carl's eye that caused Clive to keep himself awake until Carl's muffled snores began to bounce off the ceiling down to him.

Clive was up before everybody the following morning, and straight away made for the roof-garden in his dressing-gown.

'No!' he shouted, as soon as his head came above the level of the floor. The snowman's head was off. It had become a shapeless heap of snow on the ground, in which, presumably, were hidden the red ring, the eggshells and the courgette. And all over the roof-garden was fresh snow, at least two inches of it. The snow vulture was as good as new – if anything, it seemed to have grown, and its eyes to have got blacker, though that was probably Clive's angry imagination at work. He knew what he wanted to do. In fact he opened the door to go out and knock the vulture to pieces, and throw its coal-eyes over the television aerial, not caring if they hit anyone down below. But when he put one slippered foot outside, an icy gust whizzed up his pyjama leg, driving him back inside. And he knew, staring at the vulture's black eyes, that it was more than the cold that kept him from doing what he wanted to.

Instead he marched down the two flights of stairs to his bedroom and yanked Carl awake.

'What did you do that for?'

'Do what?' said a startled, sleepy Carl.

'Wreck my snowman, what do you think?'

'I never touched the stupid thing.'

'Well, who did then? That skinny, ugly snow vulture of yours?'

'Maybe,' said Carl, smiling.

'Maybe, my eye!' said Clive, and thumped Carl as hard as he could on the face. That did it. Carl swung over the side of the bed and began laying into Clive with fists and feet. Clive responded like he'd rarely done before, and soon they were on the floor, hitting and shouting, till the neighbour downstairs was banging on his ceiling with a broom, and their father was pulling them apart, their mother, whitefaced, looking on.

*

Carl had a black eye at school that day, and although it suited him, it was so unusual for him to be marked in any way that the other boys were smirking at him. So were the girls, but Carl ignored them. He scowled his way through the day, swiping at any boy who smirked too close. He made it known that he'd sleep-fallen from the top bunk and landed on his eye, but no one, not even his most faithful accomplices, believed him. The bruising on Clive's face suggested otherwise, and the whole class was amazed that Clive had come off better from the fracas. Needless to say, Clive got a bad time all day – especially after Carl saw him surrounded by boys trying to find out what the fight had been about. The fact that Clive wouldn't tell was irrelevant. Carl realized that the only way to distract them was to torture Clive, which was what he wanted to do anyway.

It was break and he knew he had ten minutes. He marched over and pushed his way through the crowd till he could grab Clive and toss him to the ground. He turned to two of his cronies.

'Hold his feet and shoulders, would you? Pin him down. The rest of you make a ring so we won't be seen.'

Clive started hollering but Carl stuffed snow in his mouth. He then opened Clive's belt and shoved handfuls of snow in his underpants, packing in as much as he could.

'If you say a word about this, I'll kill you,' he said. Then it was over. The general friendliness shown to Clive a few minutes earlier had evaporated. No one had defended him. No one was bothering to ask him now what the fight had been about.

Holding his belt Clive ran to the loo to scoop out what snow hadn't already melted. The whole middle of his body felt frozen. His underpants and pants were saturated. Of all the nasty tricks Carl had ever played on him this was one of the meanest. It was undoubtedly dangerous too. How was he going to get dry? He could hardly use it as an excuse to go home, legitimate though it might be.

He crept in, late, to the classroom, enduring the strictures of his teacher, and sat as close to the radiator as he could. Mostly he twisted his body so that as much of the wet area touched the radiator as possible, while his head looked straight ahead. It would, at the very least, give him a crick in his neck, he reckoned, but it was the lesser of two evils.

He couldn't concentrate on anything that morning except his dread of lunchtime. What would Carl organize for him then, when he'd have the luxury of an hour to play with? He could feel Carl's eyes on him from the far side of the room. He kept a close look on the clock, and five minutes from the bell he feigned a sudden attack of diarrhoea and got immediate permission to leave the room. Instead of going to the loo, however, he headed for the gym, which, fortunately, was not being used right then, and hid inside the vaulting horse to wait out the hour. It was a bit cramped but preferable to anything Carl would arrange. The hand-holes at both ends let in air. Carl would never find him here, even though, at this moment, he would be out with a gang hunting through the school. The more Clive relaxed the more hungry he felt, but if ever he was going to miss lunch it was today. He had to endure a few vaults by boys that left his head throbbing, but there weren't many. All in all, the exercise was a success.

The remainder of the schoolday passed uneventfully, mainly because Clive stayed in the classroom for the afternoon break, pretending to be working. He even managed to avoid trouble on the way home, through a strategic, last-minute missing of the bus. He hitched home quicker, getting a lift with the mother of a schoolmate. At home, he knew, Carl would try nothing serious. Before that awful brother came in, he took off his still-damp clothes and got into a hot bath.

*

Instead of putting on pyjamas and a dressing-gown, as he usually did after a bath, Clive got into clean, dry clothes. It was too early for pyjamas. Besides, he had work to do, outside work.

He went upstairs to the living-room where his mother was reading the evening paper. She glanced up as he came in.

'Are you feeling better now? Go over and stand in front of the fire and let more heat into your bones.'

She had been most surprised when he'd demanded a bath as soon as he'd got in from school. Then when she'd heard why, she'd been worried. She was always over-protective of Clive's health, and he found this tedious.

He could smell a meat pie of some sort cooking in the kitchen. He liked meat pie, especially on cold evenings. He hoped there would be broccoli with it. He knew that Carl hated that. For once he didn't glance with resentment at the television he was never allowed to watch on weekdays. It could have been smashed, with a rock in its insides, for all he cared today.

'I'm going up to the roof-garden, to build my snowman again,' he said, and headed for the stairs. His mother caught him as he passed.

'You can't go outside in the snow after a bath,' she said. 'You'll catch your death, if you haven't caught it already. Anyway you have your homework to do.'

Clive tore himself free and ran up the stairs.

'I'm alright,' he shouted from the top. 'Leave me alone. I'll do my homework later. I haven't much to do.'

'You're just as bad as your brother,' she said, as much to herself as to Clive, as he'd disappeared outside. She shook her head and went back to the paper.

Fresh snow had fallen but it wasn't falling now. The snow vulture was as solid as a statue covered in snow. It seemed to glare at Clive with its coal-eyes as if to say how dare he set foot in the roof-garden.

Clive ignored it as best he could, although he felt the cold so badly the vulture must have had something to do with it. It was as well his mother didn't realize how cold he was or she'd have had him inside and under the bedclothes quicker than you could say 'hot-water bottle'. If she hadn't been in the flat he'd have used an extension lead to rig up a fan heater on the roof-garden, to keep himself warm and at the same time melt the snow vulture.

There wasn't much time to lose if he was to get the snowman built again before dinner. He pulled the gloves from his back pocket, put them on and set to work gathering up the loose snow. This time he chose the farthest corner of the roof-garden, away from the snow vulture, right under where the clothes line started, and the hammock hooked on in summer. He worked with his hands and with his feet, and worked fast. That way he'd warm up, as well as get the thing built quicker.

Carl came charging up the stairs and cackled when he saw what Clive was at. Clive ignored him but saw, out of the corner of his eye, Carl go over and pretend to stroke the head of his vulture.

'Bad vulture,' he said, as if to a pet. Then he pointed at Clive's back.

'Eat him,' he hissed. 'Eat him.'

With more cackling he went inside, slamming the door behind him, and disappeared down the stairs.

Clive threw the snow vulture a dubious glance, then went on with what he'd been doing. He'd decided, before Carl's rude interruption, to make more of a snow bear than a snowman this time. That way it would be more capable of defending itself. He realized he was being silly as he thought this. He justified it by reasoning that the average snowman looked more like a teddybear than a man, if only because of the size of its head relative to its body. This bear would be more of a polar bear, ready to take on any vulture.

*

Something of the hostility between the twins came across to their parents at dinner. They couldn't even accidentally touch without snapping at each other. Even when they were silent it was noticeable.

Their father was in a particularly grumpy mood and let them know it.

'It's a pity I can't have a meal in peace,' he shouted. 'I've had a rough day at work. It's not too much to ask that I can relax at home.'

Carl completely ignored him and kicked Clive under the table. Their mother took a more calming line.

'Come on, boys. It's not worth it. What's it about, anyway? What did he do to you, Clive?'

'Nothing,' muttered Clive, spiking a piece of meat with his fork.

'Must be something,' his mother insisted. 'This is worse than normal.'

Carl kicked Clive again, as if to encourage him to stay quiet, and this time he got him on the ankle bone and made him yelp with pain. Their father flung his knife and fork down on his plate, spluttering gravy over the table.

'THAT'S ENOUGH,' he roared. 'I WANT QUIET.' He caught Carl by the scruff of the neck and practically threw him towards the door. 'Go down to your bedroom and stay there,' he shouted after him. Then he turned to Clive.

'If he lifts one finger to you later I want to know.' He then lapsed into a brooding silence and continued his dinner.

Clive sat quietly, eating. So did his mother. Beside

him, Carl's plate was half full. He was frightened of his father in these moods. Usually he was fun but every so often he would get as grumpy as a bear with toothache. He was worse since starting his new job. He should change jobs again if his work put him in moods like this.

At the same time Clive realized that he and Carl were partly responsible. They shouldn't fight like that all the time. It did seem like all the time recently. There must be more to a brother than someone to fight with. And weren't twins supposed to get on better with each other than ordinary brothers and sisters? If it were up to Clive there would be no fighting. Well, not much anyway. But Carl saw it differently, and it takes more than one to make peace.

Clive excused himself with great ease from the table. The mood that had settled there was so heavy that no one noticed him go. He closed the door behind him and tiptoed up to the roof-garden, having first switched the upstairs light on.

*

The body of the snow bear was waist-high, exactly as Clive had left it before dinner. Glancing at the snow vulture he was almost surprised. He continued tightly packing more snow on. Fortunately, there was plenty. The bear had to be taller, and bigger in every sense, than the vulture.

He slapped snow, almost aggressively, on the bear's shoulders and pressed it down each time, until the shoulders were as padded as an American footballer's. He took great care with the head (and put a brick from the barbecue inside, to punish head-smashers). All the time he worked fast, because the order to come inside could arrive at any moment. He raided the barbecue's charcoal for the nose, the eyes, the mouth, and the insides of the ears. He made, with great patience, the front and back legs and paws, and somehow attached them to the bear's body. The bear was sitting up. It looked so real to Clive that he thought it might amble over to the vulture, club it to the ground and devour it. If only it would.

Clive felt exhausted and, now that he'd finished working, shiveringly cold. He also felt proud, however, of his big fierce-looking bear. Carl would get a shock in the morning. Who knew what he'd see? Wasn't the polar bear known as the king of the Arctic? This snow bear was king of the roof-garden.

Clive turned with a smirk to the snow vulture, which was puny by comparison. It was the first time he'd looked its way for at least half an hour. It was almost with a start he noticed that the vulture seemed to be staring at the bear. Glaring might be a better word – he'd forgotten how evil it looked. He was sure the vulture had turned slightly while he'd been building the bear. At the same time he knew this was impossible. His mind was playing tricks on him. Nevertheless, as he looked from the bear to the vulture his earlier confidence evaporated. The bear might be bigger but the vulture radiated power. It was like a shark beside a whale.

Cold though he was, then, Clive decided he had to stay and guard his snow bear. He thought for a moment about rigging the hammock up and pulling on all the jumpers, trousers, socks he could find, and getting into one sleeping bag inside three others, but he knew he'd never be allowed. He wouldn't even be allowed to sleep inside the glass door at the top of the stairs. What could he do, then?

Well, he would leave the light on. Lights are deterrents to evil. And if he were at all inventive, he could rig up some kind of warning device that would go off if the snow bear was approached. Carl could have done it, easy. But Carl was banished to the bedroom, and, anyway, he would hardly be prepared to help Clive – especially when he realized what it was to do with.

He thought hard, shivering as he did so. It needn't be a very elaborate device. A simple bell tied to a very long piece of string would do. He could tie the end with the bell around the body of the bear, and take the other end of the string all the way down both sets of stairs to his bedroom where it would be tied to his big toe. And, winter or no winter, he'd leave the bedroom window open. That way, no matter how deeply he slept, he'd have two chances of learning about any attack on his snow bear. If he didn't hear, he'd be sure to feel his toe being tugged.

It wasn't perfect. Carl would have worked out some way of hearing directly in the bedroom, under the pillow perhaps. But it was the best Clive could think of.

With a look at the bear, as if to reassure it, Clive headed down the stairs to find a bell and string. He frightened the life out of his mother who was sitting on her own, by the fire, reading a book. She reacted as though he were a burglar, arrived by helicopter.

'Who is it? Who is it?' she said, jumping up and backing for the door.

'Clive! You've been up there all this time! Are you trying to catch pneumonia? Get down to bed at once and be thankful your father's asleep. I don't believe this!'

Clive glanced upstairs and reluctantly headed down to bed. Even inside he was frozen, especially his hands, nose and feet, so why not stay out? As he lay under the duvet with his teeth chattering, he thought of his beautiful, noble snow bear two floors directly above him. He wished houses had transparent floors. He wished he was a whizz-kid with a video camera, able to set up a night-watch. But five minutes after his mother brought him a very welcome hot-water bottle he was asleep.

*

It was late morning. Carl had gone to school but Clive was still in bed. Outside the open door of his room his mother was speaking to the doctor.

'I told him not to go up there. I warned him. I knew he'd end up like this.'

The doctor nodded his head with a little smile that showed he wasn't in the slightest interested. He pushed his glasses back on his nose and handed Clive's mother a prescription.

'Give him one teaspoonful four times a day, and keep him in bed.' He bent down and snapped his black bag shut. Then they both moved out of view towards the door of the flat.

Clive wondered if the doctor knew he'd picked up this dose, not on the roof-garden as his mother believed, but earlier in the school playground when Carl had stuffed snow in his pants. Doctors could tell anything, couldn't they? – anything to do with health. This doctor knew after a few listens on his stethoscope and a few prods on the chest that it wasn't pneumonia Clive had, only a bad dose of cold. He was probably annoyed at being called out for such a trivial matter.

Yet to Clive it didn't feel so trivial. All night long he'd sweated and tossed and turned, and snivelled and sneezed, and now his throat was sore. Just before the doctor came his mother had changed his pyjamas and the sheets on his bed, and the old ones were in the laundry basket, saturated. And behind all the suffering two things were in his mind: that Carl had done this to him; and that he'd left his snow bear on the roof-garden in the company of that snow vulture.

He wanted to do something bad to Carl, something worse than he'd ever done before. The trouble was that he couldn't think what. These things came naturally to Carl. In the area of badness Clive was a beginner.

Then at once he realized the answer was obvious. He'd smash the precious snow vulture. That would annoy Carl more than anything. Clive knew he'd tried to do it before and failed, but he had to get over his ridiculous nervousness towards the vulture. It was only made of snow. It wasn't alive. These were silly ideas Carl was putting in his head.

He thought then of his snow bear and guilt came over him. He hadn't even been up to check it this morning. It could be melted for all he knew. But, to be fair, it wouldn't have been easy for him to get up there. Apart from the fact that his mother had hardly left his room all morning – fussing around like a nurse back from retirement – he'd found his two trips to the toilet excruciatingly difficult, and the toilet was practically next door. He had no energy whatsoever.

He lay back and concentrated, and got his priorities in order. Smashing the snow vulture could wait. He was too weak for such activity. Also, he knew himself it would be dangerous, in his condition, to go out in the snow. But somehow he ought to be able to drag himself up to the door of the roof-garden, and look out to see if his bear was OK.

He decided he had to lie as still as a corpse for as long as possible. No arm or leg movements, no twitches, nothing. That way there would be a build-up of energy in the run-down battery of his body. It would be better than sleeping because his mind would be actively helping him, consciously willing the energy to flow in.

He stared at one spot in the ceiling so long that he half expected it to give way, as if under a blowtorch, and he'd find himself staring at the ceiling of the living-room. He thought of the last book he'd read and liked, one about giants, and he went back in his mind to the start of it, and imagined the story unfolding as a cartoon film on the screen of the ceiling.

Then he must have dozed off because his mother was sitting on his bed, with a bowl of steaming chicken broth on a tray, and was asking him to prop himself up with a pillow so she could feed him.

'I can feed myself,' he said, pulling himself up and realizing he felt much better. Reaching the roof-garden was a definite possibility now.

'How are you feeling, Clive? You look better.' She put her hand on his forehead and nodded. 'Temperature's gone down. Eat this hot soup and feel it working on you. We'll have you up and about in a day or so.'

She left him eating and went to get his medicine from the fridge. He was enjoying the broth. He hadn't realized, till then, how hungry he'd been. It probably would do him good too.

He decided he had to be a bit careful about his mother. It wouldn't do for her to feel he was too much recovered, else she would be in with his schoolbooks, making him work so he wouldn't fall behind. He didn't want to work.

When he'd swallowed the medicine he told her he felt very weak again, and thirsty. He asked for Lucozade, knowing there was none in.

'I'll be alright on my own till you get back,' he said.

Somewhat to his surprise she agreed to get him some. Sickness seemed to be an advantage in getting favours granted. He must remember that.

While she was getting her coat on he summoned up the tiredest look he could manage, and flopped back on the bed. But no sooner had she closed the door than he was out of bed and in his dressing-gown, and making his way slowly up the stairs.

He had no need to lie about it, he was still very weak. Already at the first landing, under the map of the moon, he had to rest. For a moment he thought about postponing the journey and going back to bed. That would be giving in, however. He struggled on.

Crossing the living-room, which seemed as big as a field, he had to stop awhile at the first armchair. It was so pleasant, lying back there, that it was a huge effort to get himself on his slippered feet again and moving. Only the knowledge that the supermarket was nearby, and his mother would be back very soon, galvanized him.

He came to the bottom of the last stairs and looked up at the panels of wire-reinforced glass. He gripped the banister tightly and set off, feeling like an arctic explorer at the end of his tether within sight of the North Pole. He took care to avoid the various flowerpots of cacti and Venus fly traps at the side of the stairs. It was a slow climb.

Eventually his head came above the wooden ledge that allowed him the first look at the roof-garden. He gripped the ledge to steady himself. His snow bear was there but, although still recognizable, it bore no comparison to how it had looked the previous evening. It had shrunk to half its size, as if a real bear had been starved for months or had most of its blood and strength sucked out. One end of the brick was poking out of its head.

The vulture was the same as before but now was bigger than the bear. All Clive's remaining energy drained away as he looked at it. He had to hold on extra tight to stop from falling backwards down the stairs. At that moment he heard the door of the flat slam shut as his mother returned from the supermarket.

*

When Carl arrived home, an unpleasant surprise was waiting for him. As he dumped his bag and bounded up the stairs to the roof-garden the surprise came to him, carried by his mother's voice.

'Come down here. You're barred from the roof-garden. Both of you are barred, till I say otherwise.'

'But why?' Carl spluttered, bending down to see her face.

'Just why,' said his mother. 'I'm fed up being a nurse and a gaoler. I'm fed up with the trouble those snowmen are causing.'

'You're being a gaoler even more by keeping me in,' Carl said. 'Anyway, they're not snowmen. One's a vulture. I don't know what the other mess is.'

'Don't be cheeky with me!' his mother said, her voice raised. 'I don't care what they are. You're finished with them. If you don't get down here this minute I'll come up and throw you down.'

She was in one of those moods, Carl thought, as he edged down with his back to the wall. It was time to be careful. It must be Clive's fault. What could Clive have done? Whatever it was, Carl didn't like it. All through the last boring English lesson at school he'd thought about his snow vulture. Clive should learn to behave.

As expected, his mother made a swipe at him as he

dodged past. She missed but knocked over a cup half-filled with cold tea that was sitting on the arm of a chair. He fairly scampered out the door before he got into more trouble. More unfair trouble, at that!

The loud mutterings of his mother followed him. She hadn't been like this for a while, and anyway it was usually he who put her into such moods. What *had* Clive done? He would go down straight away and find out.

Clive was asleep when Carl barged into the bedroom. It was disgusting, being asleep at half past four in the afternoon! There was a full glass of Lucozade on the edge of the bookshelf, losing its sparkle by the second. Carl went to drink it but remembered just in time about Clive's cold and put the glass back.

He shook Clive till he sat up.

'What did you do to put Mum in such a mood?'

'Leave me alone,' Clive said. 'I did nothing. I'm too sick to do anything.'

'You're lying. Tell me or I'll make you sicker.'

'I'm not lying. I'm not lying.'

'Did you go to the roof-garden? Is that what you did? Tell me or you'll find yourself in a wet bed.' Carl had taken the glass of Lucozade in his hand and was making as if to pour it over the duvet.

'DON'T,' Clive shouted, so loudly that Carl looked up at the ceiling, and backed away towards the window as he heard quick footsteps cross the floor above and come down the stairs.

The twins' mother charged into the room and went straight to Carl, whom she proceeded to cuff around the ears. He put his hands around his head so it didn't hurt. It never really hurt when she hit him. She was more bark than bite. Their father, now, was different.

'Can you not see Clive is sick?' she shouted. 'Yet here you are tormenting him, as usual. Isn't it enough that you didn't bother to check how he was when you came in? What kind of boy are you?'

Carl said nothing, just stood there, hunched, with his hands still around his head. He knew there would be no more. He knew she'd leave the room and go back upstairs, perhaps with a few kind words to that pathetic brother of his on the way. No, not even that. The door banged shut and the stairs were clomped on. Then footsteps went across the ceiling and the television came on.

Carl glared at Clive who was lying on his back on the bed, looking at nothing. He wanted to jump on him and punch him through the mattress, but he knew he couldn't. Any more rumpus and his mother would really make him suffer. And his father would be in from work soon. Already he was faintly worried that his mother would complain about him. He hoped there was a good television programme to distract her, but at this time of day he doubted it.

He stood at the window, in such a bad mood that he thought he would boil. Outside it was already dark. The streetlight seemed brighter because of the snow on the ground. Up there on the roof was his snow vulture with no one to tend it. He knew that, in a book, he'd open the window, shin up a drainpipe, and pull himself over the parapet of the roof-garden, but he wasn't that kind of boy. He wasn't a boy in a book, he was here in this bedroom, and there was no convenient drainpipe outside the window.

He took a last glare at his apparently sleeping brother and decided the evening was wasted. There was nothing for it but to climb into bed. He brought a book with him, and his homework to hide behind (though he had no intention of doing it). And he made as much noise climbing the ladder as he could, to interrupt Clive's sleep.

*

The next morning Clive was feeling much better when he woke, but his mother insisted he stay at home.

'You don't want a relapse,' she said. 'They're always worse than first time around.'

He couldn't see the logic of this but said nothing. He was glad enough that she was in a better mood.

She didn't even send him back to bed when he appeared in the living-room in his pyjamas and dressing-gown, trailing his duvet.

'You're looking much better today,' she said.

He nodded, turned the gas fire up, switched the television on, and settled himself on the sofa, under the duvet, with his head propped up by two cushions.

She let him do that, too. Usually she forbade the twins to watch television, except at weekends, saying there were other, better activities they could be up to, not least reading. They read plenty, even Carl. Perhaps she knew this and was relenting on the television ban to see how things went. It was more likely, however, that she was simply being extra-tolerant because Clive was unwell. And because she had been so moody yesterday.

The first programme he'd put on was boring, so he got up and switched channels. He found a study of lizards in the wild, and as he knew nothing about lizards, and there was nothing better on, he decided to watch it.

On his way back to the sofa he saw that his mother seemed to be preparing a lesson. Of course, this was one of the days she went into her school in the afternoons to work with the very young children. But then, so was tomorrow. Would she leave him alone in the flat?

He looked at the lizards moving over the desert landscape. They didn't know they were being watched, obviously. The cameraman must be using a zoom lens. Clive wouldn't mind a job like that when he grew up, going off to exotic places to make documentaries for TV. One lizard was getting suspicious, was it? It stood on a small rock, very alert, its tongue flicking in and out. Clive wondered what it would be like to have a lizard as a pet. He'd call it Boris.

It would be good if his mother did go out to work this afternoon. Why shouldn't she go? He was old enough. And today he was well enough again. She even said so. He would promise to stay in, and he *would* stay in – except for a quick visit to his bear on the roof-garden.

He got bored with the lizards, bored with

television, in fact. He switched it off and went to sit on the armchair nearest the gas fire. He went as close to the fire as he could without singeing his pyjama leg.

'You preparing for work, Mum?'

She looked up at him, surprised that he'd spoken.

'I'm preparing for the next day I go in, which will probably be tomorrow.'

Clive noted the 'probably'.

'You don't have to stay in because of me, you know. I'm not one of those tiny kids you're teaching. I'm old enough to stay in for a few hours by myself. I'm not sick any more. I'd be really happy sitting here reading my book.'

'You're only eleven. You still need looking after.'

Clive left it at that and went downstairs for his book. While he was in the bedroom he heard his mother make a phone call. He bet it was to the school. He hoped the Head would say they were desperately short-staffed. It was quite likely. No one knew better than Clive that it was cold- or flu-weather.

He returned to his seat by the fire and began reading. He really did like this book. It was an old one his mother had bought him at a second-hand market. Called *Huckleberry Finn*, it was about this wild boy a little bit older than himself, and was set a long time ago around the Mississippi River in America. At first he'd found the strange American language in it difficult to follow, but now he actually enjoyed it.

His mother asked him if he'd like scrambled eggs for brunch, and he said he would. She made good scrambled eggs. She used dried chives and basil from the roof-garden.

'Do you think you'll be alright on your own?' she asked as they ate.

'Of course,' he said, in his most grown-up manner.

'I wouldn't ask except I'm severely needed at school. And as I only do two afternoons it's not fair to miss one if I can at all help it.'

'I'll be alright. What do you think would happen to me?'

'Don't answer the door, or even the telephone. Don't sit too near the fire. Put the snib on the door as soon as I go. I'll leave the school number by the phone, so ring me if you need to, if you feel sick or anything. I'll leave as early as I can, so I'll only be away a few hours.'

After she'd washed the dishes she left, and he luxuriated in the feeling of being alone in the flat. As soon as he knew she wasn't coming back for something she'd forgotten, he headed up the stairs to the roof-garden, knowing he wouldn't like what he saw. Even so, he wasn't prepared for what he did see. There was no sign of his lovingly built bear whatsoever. Just the horrendous vulture and flat snow all around. It was as if the snow bear had never existed.

That was it! He opened the glass door and, ignoring the cold blast that gave him goose-pimples under his clothes, he marched out to where the bear had been. He rummaged with his slippered foot till he found the brick that had been in the bear's head. With this brick he pounded the vulture into smithereens, grinding the coal eyes into the snow. Then, flinging the brick on top of the pile it had come from, he went back inside.

*

Clive was very relieved that his mother was as good as her word, and was back as quickly as possible from school. Not that he'd been worried or afraid in her absence. The doorbell had rung once and he'd ignored it, though it went on ringing for a while. He'd answered the one telephone call, however. He couldn't see the sense in not doing that. Burglars and murderers couldn't climb in through the telephone wire. He'd say Mum was in the bathroom if it was someone he didn't know.

What relieved him was that his mother had got home before Carl. He didn't want to be alone when Carl discovered his vulture was gone. He had rehearsed all sorts of arguments – that the vulture had melted, that it had flown away (Carl seemed to believe it was alive anyway) – but he knew none of them would wash. He'd get a thumping. But now his mother's presence made that less likely.

She was fussing around him, making sure he was alright. As if he'd survived an ordeal!

'How was your class, Mum?' he asked, to change the subject.

'Oh, OK, but my mind was half on you.'

'Don't be silly, Mum. I was fine. I had a nice time. Oh, there was a call for you. Josey rang.'

She didn't notice that he'd broken the rule about not answering the phone. He'd thought she wouldn't. It proved it was a stupid rule.

He heard the downstairs door bang and knew Carl was home. He buried his head in his book. Stomping came up the stairs. Carl went straight across the living-room to the roof-garden's stairs. He knows, Clive thought. Look at his face.

'You could say hello to us when you get home,' their mother said.

'Hello,' Carl muttered, but kept going.

Clive glanced up over the edge of his book, preparing himself for the explosion. Perhaps, in his anger, Carl would fall down the stairs and break his neck. No, he didn't want that. But he didn't want a thumping either.

There was silence. Then Clive heard the unmistakable sound of the door to the roof-garden opening, and Carl going out. This was remarkable control on Carl's part. Most uncharacteristic. He was a changed boy. What had happened?

Clive strained his ears but could hear nothing. Only his mother scraping carrots behind him in the kitchen. He felt a great urge to go upstairs and look out, but he didn't move. He didn't trust Carl. It could be an ambush. Carl could be waiting for him outside that glass door, ready to pull him out and pummel him into the snow.

He forced himself to go on reading, but the lines of print went flying across his eyes. He could concentrate on nothing. Once again the urge came to check out the roof-garden. He went, instead, into the kitchen.

'Need any help, Mum? Is there anything I can do?'

'You can wash that pile of dishes,' she said, tears running from her eyes from the onions she was slicing. 'That would be a help.'

He set to work, this time quite gladly, though normally he'd do anything to avoid it. He only liked washing up when he was depressed or distracted, and wanted to waste time in some mindless way.

As usual, he had too many suds, and couldn't see his hands under water. He splashed away, smelling his mother's cooking. It was a curry of some sort, vegetable he thought. He liked that, as long as it wasn't too hot. Everyone in the family liked that.

Carl was directly above him. He glanced over at the window where the end of a green hose for watering the plants on the roof-garden hung. The other end of that hose was up there. For a moment Clive wondered if he could look into his end of hose and see, as if through a periscope, a view of the roof-garden. He shook his head and continued washing.

What was Carl doing up there all this time? Was he not cold? He'd only had his jacket on when he went up there. Clive looked at his mother. She didn't seem bothered. She was busy sprinkling spices into the saucepan.

He left the dishes drip-drying, and walked towards the stairs to the roof-garden. He began to climb. Up, until his head came above the wooden ledge and he could see out. What did he see? He saw Carl sitting on the pile of bricks that he'd dusted the snow off. And beyond Carl was the snow vulture, looking exactly like it had done before Clive had demolished it.

*

Clive did so much thinking that night he thought his brain would burn through his skull. His light was off. Carl was asleep. Clive couldn't sleep yet if he tried.

He was thinking of the vulture. The snow vulture that had resurrected, had built itself again from the scattered snow. At least, this was what he first thought. What else would explain Carl's lack of reaction when he'd gone up to the roof-garden first? He was only human. If he'd seen no vulture there he'd have made a lot of noise.

Or would he? Although he wasn't up there long, he could, Clive supposed, have had time to build it again. He'd taken much longer the first time, but the second time he knew exactly what he was doing. Yet it wasn't really long enough, was it? And the vulture looked identical to how it had looked before. That would surely have been impossible to manage in a short time, from memory too.

Still, that was the most logical interpretation. The vulture was made of snow. Clive had to keep reminding himself of this.

It was all Carl's doing, of course. He knew exactly what was, or was not, going on. His non-reaction on the roof-garden this evening had been very cunning. If the snow vulture wasn't alive, Carl was doing his best to convince Clive it was.

There was only one thing for it. Clive had to forget about the vulture. It would take a conscious effort but he'd do it. It was Carl's creation. Like a spider with its web, Carl had sucked Clive into his obsession. And Carl was enjoying this.

Clive decided, suddenly, that he'd have to find a

new obsession of his own. Some fascinating hobby to put all his spare time into. Well, not all. He still wanted to read. But something different that was his alone.

He didn't know what it would be yet, but he felt good about his decision. He chuckled a little, looking up at the slats above him, between which Carl's mattress could be seen. He had a feeling he would easily come up with this new, exciting hobby. He turned over on his side to sleep on it, giving a last goodbye thought to the snow vulture. And another thought followed this. The snow wouldn't last much longer. The vulture's days were numbered. Whatever Clive thought of would have nothing to do with snow.

*

All through school the next day Clive was distracted. He had an idea on the go that he liked the feel of. It began with wood. It had something to do with model airplanes. It had a little to do with building snowmen, or snow bears. But it was all a bit mixed up.

He took it slowly. He ignored, as much as possible, the history video (though he couldn't ignore it completely because he knew there would be follow-up work). He went back in his mind to his model airplanes. He didn't build them any more, but he'd loved the building of them, especially the use of glue. In the end he'd tried making them without looking at the instructions.

He'd enjoyed making the snow bear too, and that was more recent. And he liked wood. It was very simple, really. He'd build something in wood. A wooden man, a wooden bear, he didn't know yet. He was very excited at the thought. It would be like sculpture. What size would it be? Not too big and not too small, he reckoned. About a metre high maybe. And where would he get the wood? What form would this wood take?

He suddenly thought of matches! They were common enough, and easy to come by. How many thousand did they go through at home in a year? The gas cooker, the gas fire were both lit with matches (even though the gas fire was supposed to be automatic). Not to mention his mother's awful smoking habit.

That was it, that's what he'd do. This evening when he went home he'd start collecting spent matches in a box. He'd snap off the burnt bits, of course. They'd all be different sizes but that wouldn't matter. He'd have to be patient in the beginning but he could manage that. On Friday when he got his pocket money he'd buy glue.

Would it not be better to buy a big box of matches too? Make it all with unused matches? He remembered once going to lunch with his parents, to an artist friend of theirs, and seeing this amazing wood sculpture hanging from the ceiling, charred black. The artist had explained that it had been made from matches which he'd lit when the sculpture was finished. Clive remembered being astonished that the sculpture hadn't burned away.

But Clive was no professional artist, no grown-up either. His parents would never allow him to use unused matches, even the brown safety type. He needed their consent, too, if only to keep Carl from wrecking his sculpture. He'd stick with the used matches. It would be slower, but he was in no real hurry.

He was aware that the video was over, and the teacher was standing in front of him.

'Clive,' the teacher said, 'maybe you'd like to tell us about the Battle of Hastings.'

*

Although he'd never admit it, Carl was secretly tired of his snow vulture. At the same time he was proud that something he'd built looked so good and lasted so long. But enough was enough – especially now that Clive wasn't bothered by it any more.

It was Saturday morning, and he was up on the roof-garden, alone with the snow vulture. He stared at it, wondering how it could possibly have survived so long. There was practically no other snow on the roof-garden, apart from in the corners or at the base of the walls. He wanted to think it was because the vulture was so well built, but he couldn't really believe that. Snow everywhere was melting fast, yet his vulture hadn't even lost an eye or shrunk a centimetre.

OK, it was built right against a wall and that would give it shelter. But shelter didn't really affect temperature. He peered closely at the vulture's face as if the answer might be there but he learned nothing. All he saw was expertly shaped snow and coal.

He thought of Clive, downstairs in the bedroom, lying on his mouth and nose on the floor, with a spread newspaper underneath him. He had glue and matches.

'What are you doing?' Carl had asked him.

'I'm making something,' Clive had replied.

'What are you making?'

'None of your business. Go off to your snow vulture.'

Carl had gone off, only because he didn't want his curiosity to show. At the same time he noticed that Clive had got cheekier towards him in recent weeks. This had to stop.

Perhaps Clive had more to do with the vulture than he pretended. Perhaps he kept it for periods in the freezer. Or, if that was too difficult, perhaps he had a supply of snow somewhere that he used to patch up the vulture whenever a bit melted or fell off. He would have sensed by now that Carl was tired of his creation. No, it wouldn't do. Much as he liked the idea, he didn't really believe it. It would be too convenient to have Clive to blame. There was something different going on here, something simpler, no doubt. The vulture was just a freak of the weather. It would be gone very soon.

He went inside and closed the glass door behind him. He thought about going down to annoy Clive at his silly match-glueing game but his father had warned him about that over breakfast. Typical of Clive, Carl thought, running to Dad or Mum for protection! He wasn't worth bothering with. Instead, Carl went down to see what was on television.

*

Carl watched as Clive applied glue to another match, and stuck this to the fragile construction on the newspaper. It would have been so easy to break it into bits. Even when the glue dried, it would be easy. Carl was tempted.

The shape on the newspaper was roughly like the sole of a shoe.

'It's a man you're making, isn't it?' he asked.

'Wow, you're some detective,' Clive said.

'A bit obvious, isn't it, making a man?'

'That's what you said when we went to build things in the snow. This is different, and you know it. How many match-men have you made? How many have you seen?'

'I haven't seen one here yet. There's a long way to go from making the sole of a foot to making a man. How are you going to get it to stand, or even to stay together?'

'I'll manage, don't worry.'

'We'll see about that. I'll bet you'll get fed up with the whole thing very soon. And if you don't, and it does stay together, make sure you lock it up when you're not here!'

'If you touch it, you'll be sorry.'

'Ha, ha, that's a laugh. You and whose army?'

'Me and Dad, that's who.'

'You always have to bring Mum or Dad into it, don't you? You can't do anything on your own. You're a big baby.'

'That's right. Why don't you bring your vulture down to scare me with? Your vulture that you made all on your own.'

'Leave my vulture out of it.'

'What's the matter, Carl? Are you getting bored with your snow vulture? Gone off it, have you? I can't believe it.'

'You're just jealous, that's all. The stupid things you built in snow didn't last.'

'I couldn't care less about your silly snow vulture. I have better things to bother about.'

'If better things is what you call that junk you're making, you can keep your better things.'

'Suits me. Now, if you'll please leave me alone . . .'

'I wouldn't stay if you paid me,' said Carl, and stormed out of the room, banging the door behind him.

He was fuming. He didn't usually let Clive get to him like that. Clive and his stupid glued matches! What did he care? He went up to the sitting-room. Mum was out. Dad was watching a football match on telly, an international, England versus Germany. Carl saw another row looming there, as he didn't support the same side as his dad, and he suspected his dad's side would win. There was nothing for it but another trip to the roof-garden. Why didn't they live in a mansion with rooms to get lost in? He headed up the stairs he was beginning to dislike, up to look for signs of melting.

*

The sun was shining. A weak sun, admittedly, but still a sun. Shoots would be showing in the flowerpots soon. It was nearly time to get out the hammock and hang it in the roof-garden. The corners were free of snow. Yet the snow vulture was still there.

Carl stood in the doorway, looking out at it. He was thoroughly fed up with it. He was sorry he'd ever made it. He'd built a monster, something unnatural, obscene. Why had this happened? All he'd done was shape some snow.

And Clive was irritating him more and more – both with his cynical comments about the vulture, and with the little man he was building out of matches. Already he had half a leg.

There was nothing else for it. Carl knew he had to smash the vulture. Whatever freak reason there was for it not melting wouldn't apply to loose scattered snow. In half an hour there would be no snow on the roof-garden.

He glanced down the stairs to see if Clive was there. It wouldn't do for *him* to see this. He then looked around for something to hit the vulture with. The mop for the kitchen floor was there, standing on its end against the glass wall. That would do. On second thoughts, he didn't need it. He'd kick the vulture to bits. That was what he felt like doing anyway.

He went out and closed the door behind him. He went over to the vulture, drew his right foot back and let fly. The pain! It was as if he'd kicked a statue! The vulture was solid! Carl was on the ground, holding his foot.

Had he broken it? The pain was terrible. He took his shoe and sock off and examined the foot, wiggling the toes this way and that. Nothing seemed to be broken. It didn't feel that way.

He glared at the vulture. The kick hadn't taken a chip out of it. How was it so hard? It couldn't be snow any more. He shakily reached out a hand and touched its base. It was cold and slippery alright, like iced snow. Yet that was impossible in such mild weather as this. And even ice broke up under a kick.

Mild weather or no mild weather, Carl's bare foot was cold. He put the sock and shoe on again and retreated inside, banging the glass door behind him but making sure to lock it. He took a last glance at the vulture as he went down the stairs.

I'm not beaten yet, he thought. I'll be back. You wait and see.

*

Carl was unrecognizable at school on Monday. He seemed distracted. He had no time for his rough friends, even at break. At lunchtime he did something he'd never done before – he went to the library and spent the whole hour there.

He asked the librarian to show him where he'd find books about ice and snow. He took four books over to a table and set about going through them quickly but carefully. He was looking at the properties of snow, especially under strange conditions. He wanted to know if it could go hard, as hard as his vulture. In the classroom this morning he'd come up with a theory: that under mild conditions firmly packed snow would fuse together, and the snow would get harder the longer it survived. The fact that his vulture was the only example he'd ever seen that fitted this theory didn't disprove it. But he found nothing in the books to support it. Nothing at all.

He put the books back on the shelf and returned to the classroom. They had science last lesson. He could ask his science teacher privately. No, he wouldn't do that. What would the science teacher know about snow that wasn't in the four books?

On the bus home he sat down roughly beside Clive, knocking him against the window.

'Hey, do you mind!' said Clive, rubbing his shoulder.

Carl said nothing, just stared moodily ahead. Clive caught him by the arm and said in a loud whisper, 'Do you mind, I said. That hurt!'

'Sorry,' muttered Carl, as if it was the last thing he meant. Then he turned and noticed Clive. 'Look, I didn't mean it, OK?'

Clive went on rubbing his shoulder with a sulky look as Carl took a packet of crisps out of his pocket and started eating. He didn't pull the bag away as Clive reached out and took a few. He even, to Clive's surprise, absent-mindedly moved the bag in Clive's direction. There was something on his mind, that was obvious. Clive reached for some more crisps before the mood wore off.

Going to overtake, the bus braked so suddenly they went into the back of the seat in front of them. Even then, Carl didn't react, though Clive was yelling with most of the other kids.

'What's bugging you?' Clive said suddenly to Carl.

'Nothing's bugging me. Leave me alone.'

'Nothing! I know you. What is it?'

Carl looked at Clive as if looking for the traces of a sneer. 'OK, I have a problem.'

'Go on, what is it?'

'No, I won't tell you. I don't need your help.'

'Suits me,' said Clive, and turned to look out the window.

'It's the snow vulture,' said Carl. 'It won't melt.'

Clive laughed and shook his head. 'Look, I told you, I'm not interested in your snow vulture. If that's your problem you can keep it.'

'But I don't understand it. How can it still be here?'

'Maybe you made it too well.'

'Don't be smart, Clive. I'm worried. It's gone hard, like stone, only it's still cold. I tried to kick it to bits and it nearly broke my foot. It's not right.'

'OK, it's not right, but why worry? Think of it as a statue. A roof-garden vulture instead of a garden gnome. You liked it enough when you made it first.'

'Stop being funny. You're being very helpful, aren't you?'

'Very. Maybe I learned it from you.'

They went silent then. Clive looked out the window at the houses going by, some of them with trees outside, most with cars. He was more sympathetic than he was pretending to be. It was very puzzling, and he could see Carl was unusually upset. But Carl had been nasty to him for so long. He wasn't going to forgive him that easily.

When they got home Carl shut himself in the bedroom. Clive, out of curiosity, went to the roof-garden to see for himself. The vulture looked the same as it had done when he'd last seen it. And yet, as Carl had said, the temperature didn't seem low enough.

Clive pressed firmly with his thumb against the vulture's nose, but it wouldn't budge. It was cold, too, like something taken from the freezer. What was going on here? For a moment he thought of taking a brick and bashing it again, but he remembered what Carl had said about kicking it and almost breaking his foot. Also, he knew that it was after he'd used the brick last time that the vulture had grown tough. Just as a second toenail is very tough after you lose the first.

But it wasn't his problem. What had happened to his resolution to ignore it? As long as it stayed there, on the roof-garden, it wasn't harming anyone. Carl had to learn to forget it.

He closed the door and went downstairs to raid the ashtrays for matches. He was forgetting he had a growing man to feed.

*

Carl avoided the roof-garden for a few days, in the hope that when he went back up there the snow vulture would show signs of melting. That was all he wanted, a little slimming on the vulture's part. A lost eye or something. He knew better than to expect to find the vulture completely gone.

He tried to forget it altogether but couldn't. As a result he wasn't himself, either at home or at school, and people noticed. He knew they were talking about him behind his back. He also knew that if he went on this way he was in danger of losing friends.

He asked himself what exactly was bothering him. Was he afraid the vulture might do something to him, turn against its creator? He didn't think so. After all, it hadn't moved a centimetre from the day it was built. Or had it? What about the fate of Clive's snowman and snow bear?

He shook his head to clear it of that thought. That vague thought. They'd probably simply melted. Wasn't his vulture showing now that it was immune to melting, that it was somehow different to other snow creatures and therefore subject to different laws?

It was this difference itself, surely, that was worrying Carl. He liked things clear and logical. It disturbed him if they weren't – and this was way beyond the bounds of anything he understood, or had experienced before. And somewhere at the back of his mind was the feeling that, because it had happened to him, he was responsible. But how, or why, he couldn't see.

During these days Clive found Carl preoccupied and different, but not quite in a bad mood. This was a relief, as constructing his match-man was a delicate business, and any interruption would make it impossible. The normal Carl would have broken up the match-man or, worse still, stuck matches on it himself any old way, thereby ruining Clive's work. Clive would have had to find lockable hiding places to work in, such as the bathroom, and that would have caused countless problems. It was much easier to lie on the floor, as he could do now, and not bother about anything but his building.

The match-man was going well. Clive was very organized in his match-gathering. He had a heavy brown paper bag pinned to the cork board in the kitchen, on which he'd printed, in big black letters, SPENT MATCHES. He'd asked his friends to save matches in their homes for him. His patience was continuing to hold up, although it had given way once when he'd found a ten pence piece on the carpet, and had bought a box of matches with it. He cut all the brown tops off, of course, with heavy scissors, and put them in a plastic bag which he tied and left in the bin. That night he'd worried about the bin going on fire, but it didn't.

He'd finished the left leg by now, and it did look good. It wasn't a matter of one cuboid stuck to another longer one. He could have slipped a shoe onto the foot, so right did it look. And the leg, although it wasn't round, was narrower at the bottom than at the top, and even bulged a bit at the knee. All in all, Clive was extremely proud of his match-leg. He left it standing, by itself, on top of his desk under the window, where it was best admired.

He allowed himself a little rest before he went on to the next part. Wasn't the human body a convenient shape when it could be copied in parts? He thought for a while of carrying on up the left side, or jumping to the head, even, but in the end he decided against it. The head would be difficult to get right. Better to wait till he was more practised. Even proceeding up the left side would be silly. He would do the right leg next, as was obvious, and he would take it from there.

Carl ignored Clive's construction. He ignored most things during these days, just kept to himself, joining the others for his meals, which he only picked at anyway. One morning, before breakfast, he went up to the roof-garden again. The snow vulture looked exactly as before. This did not surprise Carl. He opened the door, went out and walked slowly round the vulture. He was convinced that he saw, out of the corner of his eye, the vulture move its head as he circled it.

*

Clive was with his parents at the breakfast table. It was Saturday, so the breakfast was leisurely. At Clive's request, they were having frankfurters and beans. He was even cooking the meal himself. The tea was already made, and on the table.

He had called Carl once, and now did so again. They would be able to eat in a few minutes. He liked cooking. He knew he could only do simple things yet, but he had to start somewhere.

'It's strange,' his mother said to his father, 'but none of the spring plants are showing on the roof-garden yet. I set all the usual seeds in good time, the flowers and the herbs, and there's nothing visible.'

'It's very early in the year,' said his father.

'With this mild weather? Come on, there should be one or two shoots growing.'

'Aren't you forgetting the snow we had?'

'Oh, that snow didn't last long. Apart from that, we've had the mildest of winters.'

Clive was listening to this while he was putting the

food out on plates. If what his mother was saying was true, then he blamed the vulture. Nothing good would come of it. At the same time, he knew very little about plants. Wouldn't snow, for example, kill them anyway?

He supposed his mother knew what she was talking about. Just before he sat down to eat he went to call Carl a third time, but Carl walked into the kitchen, already dressed.

'How is your wooden man coming along?' his father asked Clive. Clive had his mouth full, and had to chew furiously before he could answer. He hated talking while he was eating. Especially when he'd cooked the meal himself.

'It's going good,' he said. 'I've one leg made.'

'One leg, only? You call that good?'

'It's very fiddly work, you know. You couldn't do it.'

'When do I get to see this wonderful leg?'

'When it's on the man. I'm not letting anyone see any bits till it's finished.'

'At this rate, we'll have a long wait,' his father said with a chuckle.

He then turned his attention to Carl, who had barely muttered a good morning as he'd sat down.

'I see you have your own sculpture already finished. A white bird. And very clever it is, too, because it looks like snow. Your mother tells me you made one earlier out of snow. What's the new one made out of? Plastic?'

Carl nodded, looking over at Clive. Clive had stopped eating for the moment.

'How did you make it, Carl?'
'I made it at school.'
'Did you have help?'
'Yes.'
'It's a nice trick,' his father said. Then, to Clive, he said, 'Maybe you should finish your wooden man at school. That way you'll finish it before you're married.'
Clive stared at Carl again, before going back to his breakfast, but Carl didn't take his eyes off his plate. That was a close one, Clive thought. Imagine Dad thinking the vulture was a sculpture. Presumably Clive's match-man had given him the idea. Otherwise the questions would have been a bit harder to answer.
But maybe Carl would have preferred it that way. He was worried about the vulture's continuing presence. He needed help and that would have been an easy way of asking for it. Why didn't he come straight out with the truth anyway? Clive knew, however, that Carl knew that their parents wouldn't believe it.
Possibly they didn't believe the vulture was a sculpture either. Possibly they were being nice to Carl because he was down in the dumps. Yet what did they think that thing on the roof was, if it wasn't a sculpture?

*

In the afternoon the twins' mum and dad went out shopping. They invited Clive and Carl to go with them but neither wanted to go. Clive's reason was his match-man, but when he tried to work at it he couldn't concentrate.

Carl was on his mind. All his brother's badness had faded for Clive because it was so long since he'd seen any. It was only a week, but a week in the depressed state Carl was in was a long time. Long enough, almost, to forget Carl was ever any other way.

Almost, but not quite. What bothered Clive about Carl now was that Carl had become a bore. He never spoke, he never did anything. It was as if he was asleep. Clive never thought he'd miss Carl's bad behaviour, but he did. At least Carl was alive then. Even at his worst, all he needed was to be toned down a little.

So, because of this, and also because of the growing sympathy he felt for Carl, Clive decided to help him.

He went upstairs to where Carl was watching the television without interest.

'Let's get the vulture,' Clive said.

Carl was surprised. Clive's simple statement took a minute to sink in. Then he was on his feet, switching the television off.

'How are we going to do it?' Carl asked.

'We'll smash it, of course.'

'But I told you what happened when I kicked it.'

'We'll use a brick, like I did when I smashed it before.'

'You did?'

'Don't give me that, Carl. Remember that day I was off sick, and you came home from school and went up and built the vulture again without saying anything.'

'But I didn't. It wasn't smashed.'

'You're lying, Carl.'

The sight of the vulture through the glass stopped the argument. It wouldn't be there for long, Clive thought. A foot was one thing, a brick was another. This time he'd sweep all the snow up and flush it down the toilet.

They opened the door and Clive picked a brick up immediately and approached the vulture. Carl just stood watching. Clive hit the vulture hard on the head with the brick. Nothing happened, not even white dust. He hit the head again. Again, nothing happened, except that Clive's hand hurt.

He looked at Carl and saw a frightened look in his eyes. This annoyed him. He could do with a touch of the old Carl right now. He chucked the brick back on the pile and went in to the tool-box under the stairs, and came back with a hammer.

He took a run at the vulture and hit it an almighty swipe with the hammer but all that happened was that a loud crack went out over the rooftops, and Clive thought his arm had come off. There was no visible crack on the vulture. He felt it with his fingers to make sure but it was as smooth as ice, and as cold. How was this possible? What was it made of? Some super-tough form of ice? But even stone would chip if hit with a hammer.

He remembered the cold on his fingers and suddenly went downstairs to the airing cupboard where the hair-drier was kept. It was a very powerful hair-drier. As he got the extension lead out he thought to himself: let's see how it copes with this.

He switched the hair-drier on full power and held it

right against the vulture's chest. It would burn through a human chest, he reckoned, but, again, it did nothing against the vulture. As a last attempt, he boiled a kettle of water and emptied this over the vulture, taking care not to scald himself. He might as well have sprinkled it with crushed ice.

When later that afternoon the twins' parents found both boys in the same glum mood they looked at each other, and one of them suggested they turn around and go out again.

*

First thing Sunday morning Clive noticed a change in Carl. He had that determined, aggressive look on his face once again, and it was no surprise when he snapped at Clive while they were both dressing. Clive didn't bother to reply, not even through the door that Carl banged on his way out.

After that Clive took his time going upstairs. He sat on the bed and waited. It was going to be like old times, he knew it was. Yes, there were the raised voices in the kitchen. Carl, then Mum, and finally, very loudly, Dad. Then the predictable stomping across the living-room to switch on the television so loud that Clive could hear it was a church service, something Carl wasn't interested in watching anyway. He did it for badness, as everyone knew, but because it was church no one said anything. Except for the inevitable command to turn the volume down.

The old Carl was back, make no mistake about it. He was so much back that it was difficult to believe he'd ever been away. So much for Clive's missing Carl's bad behaviour.

The pretended interest in the church service wouldn't last long. Very shortly, Clive knew, Carl would be down to give him trouble. And that trouble would very likely be a broken match-man. Clive looked over at what he'd already built. The completed left leg would have to be hidden, certainly. The half-made foot of the right leg didn't matter so much.

He looked around the room and decided that nowhere in there was safe. Carl would up-end the room looking for it. Wherever he hid the match-leg it would be found. It was Carl's room too, after all.

He thought about possible hiding places outside the room. For a moment the roof-garden was enticing, in behind the bay tree maybe. Carl would never go up there now. But when Clive thought of the reason why, and the image of the vulture being whacked with a hammer came into his mind, he decided against the roof-garden.

Besides, he'd have to go through the living-room to get up there. Better to stay on the floor he was on. There had to be somewhere down here. Somewhere obvious, yet surprising at the same time. What about the airing cupboard?

He went to check it out. The obvious disadvantage was the heat from the pipes. There wouldn't be much to be gained from preventing Carl finding the match-leg, if its glue was melting all the while it was hidden.

He rummaged in the bottom, well away from the pipes. The water-tank itself was so thickly insulated that it felt barely warm. Down there on the floor were old blankets, rags, a lilo, and a sleeping-bag no one used any more. He quickly got the match-leg, wrapped it in a blanket, and stuck it in the sleeping-bag which he buried at the bottom of the heap. It wasn't absolutely safe here, he knew, but it was the best he could think of in a hurry. He hoped it worked.

His mother was calling him to the telephone. One of his friends from school, she said. With a last look at where the leg was hidden, he closed the airing cupboard door and bounded upstairs. It might be an invitation to a party.

*

The half-made right foot was still in one piece. The trouble was, there was a whole bag-load of matches stuck to it in a shapeless heap, and although the glue wasn't quite dry, it would be messy, if not impossible to separate the foot.

Clive sat on his hunkers in front of it, fuming. Well, it was more pretend fuming than real fuming, although he certainly wasn't pleased. But he knew that he'd left the foot there deliberately, almost as a sacrificial victim, to deflect Carl from the left leg he'd worked so long at. Still, he couldn't let on to Carl.

His drawers were pulled open, and his clothes had been messed about, so he knew Carl had looked for the leg. For a moment he felt the panicky urge to run out to the airing cupboard and check. Instead he turned to face Carl who was lounging on the top bunk, staring moodily at the ceiling.

'You ruined my man, why?'

'I just helped it along.'

'You leave my things alone, do you hear me?'

'Go climb up a lamppost.'

'Don't get smart with me, and don't ever do anything like this again.'

Clive suddenly picked up the now grotesque foot, and, standing on the edge of his bed, shoved it in Carl's face. He felt the new matches give way and the still soft glue spread everywhere.

'Keep it then, now that you've wrecked it.'

He then left the room and went upstairs to where his newspaper-reading parents would keep the peace.

As he sat there, not watching the television that he'd switched on, he felt pleased with his show of anger. It was important that Carl believed he'd riled him. Clive understood that Carl was getting at him only because he couldn't destroy the vulture. And he understood that Carl had come out of his earlier, demoralized state in the only way he knew how, which was to be nasty to people.

It was probably better for Carl, but it would be worse for Clive. How, for example, would he get his match-man built?

*

For the next few days Carl was so obnoxious at home and at school that Clive avoided him as much as he could. It was impossible to avoid him completely, however, as he found out in the school playground one day when he was beaten up, almost under the nose of a teacher. Other boys were being attacked as well, even some of Carl's onetime friends. It was a wonder, Clive thought, that they didn't all gang up on Carl.

It was beginning to look as if the grown-ups were doing just that. Not only was Carl in trouble with his teachers, inevitably, and with the Head, but they had got in touch with his parents. This would have come as no surprise to his parents, as answering back and sullen insolence was what they had come to expect from Carl recently. It didn't help them be patient with him, however.

So punishment at home and at school became the order of the day for Carl. It didn't curb his nastiness, Clive noticed, but this brought more punishment down on Carl, until his time and opportunities for nastiness were extremely limited. He spent a lot of his time at home banished to the bedroom, which was mostly a good thing, but at bedtime Clive had to go in there. It was like sleeping in a panther's cage.

He consoled himself with the uninterrupted use (once dinner was over, and his homework was done) of the kitchen table to build his match-man on. He spread newspaper there first, of course. Then he painstakingly stuck matches on, one at a time, sitting back every now and then to rest his fingers and take stock of his progress. Occasionally his father came in to check him out and mutter encouragement but never, fortunately, to give advice. Mostly, however, his parents ignored him.

Which was just as well, Clive thought. He was enjoying making his own decisions about how to proceed with his match-sculpture. He was close to finishing the second leg now, and was very excited about the prospect of starting on the torso. Every so often, however, the black mood from downstairs would come like a smell through the floor and spoil his enjoyment. He took care, every night, to conceal his work in the airing cupboard.

Even though he dreaded going down to the bedroom, he still felt sorry for Carl. He alone knew what was behind Carl's current mood. As far as his parents and the others were concerned, this was just Carl being worse than usual. Clive hoped it wouldn't last much longer. He knew that if it did, expulsion and worse would occur.

Carl should tell his parents about the vulture. That was what Clive thought. He knew it would be hard to convince them. But what was the alternative? Anything had to be better than the situation that now existed.

He decided he would try to persuade Carl to do this, no matter what Carl called him or did to him in the process. He packed up his match-sculpture, left it in its hiding place, and marched decisively into the bedroom.

He was not prepared for what he saw. Carl was cowering against the wall in his top bunk with the duvet over his head. He seemed to be shaking.

'What's the matter, Carl?' Clive asked, closing the door behind him.

'It's here,' the muffled voice replied.

'What's here?' Clive asked, looking round. 'There's nothing here.'

'The vulture, over there by the window.'

'There's no vulture here. Come out and see for yourself.'

Carl very reluctantly took the duvet from his head and looked. He turned to a disbelieving Clive.

'It was there, I swear to you. And it's not the first time I've seen it.'

'Come off it, Carl. A snow vulture that won't melt is one thing, but one that flies, and comes through walls, is another.'

'One thing is as strange as the other,' Carl said. 'It was here, I'm telling you. I've seen it in the bathroom too, and at school one day. It's haunting me.'

'You're imagining it. You need to see a doctor.'

'I knew you'd say that. That's what Mum and Dad would say. You mustn't tell them.'

'Why not? It's the only sensible thing to do. This has all got too much. What are you going to do?'

'I don't know. I don't know yet. I'm tired. Let me sleep.'

Clive shrugged and went out to the bathroom. He decided to run a bath. He needed somewhere alone to sit and think.

*

Three times he had to let some of the water out and replace it with hot. And twice there was a knock on the door from someone who wanted in. He couldn't hog the bathroom much longer. Whoever had decided in the first place that bathrooms and toilets should be combined was a nincompoop. It was even more amazing that this idea should have been taken up.

He rubbed some soap on the sponge and started to scrub himself. It was almost an afterthought. The longer he stayed in the bath the more likely he was to forget to wash himself. It was a wonder he'd never fallen asleep in the bath.

No chance of that happening in this flat, he thought, as someone rapped on the door again. It was his mother this time.

'Come on, Clive, you've been in there for ages. There's more than you living here, you know.'

'OK, OK, I'm coming,' he said, splashing himself all over to get the soapsuds off. With the other hand he leaned over and pulled the stopper out. Immediately a whirlpool was set up, through which the soapy water noisily escaped. Where to, Clive suddenly wondered? Alright, he knew about sewers but he had never been down there, and had no real picture of what they looked like. And where did the sewers end up? In the sea, where all the fish were? Whose crazy idea was this in the first place?

The door handle rattled again.

'Please hurry,' his mother's voice said. She couldn't have been back upstairs since the last time. Clive was by now out of the bath and busy with the towel.

'You can dry yourself in the bedroom,' she said.

He reluctantly opened the door and was no sooner out when it was banged shut behind him.

He stayed there, in the corridor, till he was dry and dressed in pyjamas and dressing-gown, with the towel a damp mess on the carpet. He didn't want to go into the room to Carl till he'd sorted his thinking out, gone over again what thoughts had come to him in the bath. Of course, it would have been better if he'd stayed in the bath, but evictions were evictions.

One thing seemed clear to him: there was a direct connection between Carl's badness and the problems with the vulture. He didn't know how, and, in fact, the continuing existence of the vulture and its changed physical make-up were both impossible, but it was up there on the roof-garden, indestructible as iron. And even Carl wouldn't deny that it was nourished on, and made strong by, badness. Now it had turned on its creator. Or so Carl would have him believe. This brought in the main thought from his interrupted time in the bath: that Carl must be having hallucinations, like advanced gangrene patients have. He remembered his dad telling him about being in a hospital ward for a few weeks once when he was a student, and about an old farmer (who had gangrene) in the bed opposite seeing his dog and sheep in the room. Carl couldn't have gangrene but there were other ways to get hallucinations. The super-hardening of the snow vulture was difficult to explain, but with pollution and damage to the ozone layer, and awful new diseases with no cure for them yet, there would be a lot more disturbing things happening that had never happened before. Maybe, at this moment, in different parts of the world, several snowmen were surprising their builders by hardening and refusing to go away.

His mother emerged from the bathroom to find him still outside the door.

'What are you doing here? Are you daydreaming,

or something? Go and put that wet towel in the laundry basket, then get into bed.'

As he bent down to pick up the towel she gave him a kiss, and said in a gentler voice, 'You gave me a shock when I came out and found you here. Goodnight, Clive.'

''Night, Mum,' he said after her as she went up the stairs.

When he got into his room he was disappointed to find Carl asleep. He went to wake him but decided that what he had to tell Carl could wait. Carl wouldn't like it much anyway. Clive didn't feel at all sleepy, so he crept out to the airing cupboard to unearth his unfinished matchstick man. All this thinking about Carl's vulture had made him neglect his own beautiful creation. It wasn't fair.

*

At school the next day, during lunchbreak, Clive came across Carl cowering in the toilets. He only found him because he went looking for him, having missed him everywhere.

'Carl?' he said, outside the locked door of a cubicle.

The question was unnecessary, as Clive had seen it was Carl by standing on the toilet seat in the next cubicle and looking over. Carl had been sitting there, fully clothed, looking miserable.

'Carl,' he said again. 'Why don't you answer? It's me, Clive.'

'Go away,' Carl muttered.

'Come on, Carl. Talk to me. You asked me to help you. I'm ready to try. Come out of there.'

'It's no good. No one can help.'

Clive didn't like the sound of this. He tried a joke, the kind Carl usually went in for.

'Come on, Carl. You're blocking a toilet someone will need to use in the next few minutes. It's after lunch, you know, and beans were on the menu – as usual.'

'Tough,' said Carl, without feeling.

'Carl, this is stupid,' Clive said, with a great deal of irritation. 'I hate talking through doors. What are you hiding from anyway?'

'It's here,' Carl said. 'I saw it.'

'What's here? The vulture? Don't be ridiculous!'

'I definitely saw it, as we came out to the playground. It was sitting there, on a branch of the tree by the school entrance. And it was staring at me.'

'You're imagining it. There's nothing there. Come out and I'll go there with you right now to prove it.'

'No, no, I won't go there.'

'Well, you'll have to come out and make your way back to the classroom, as the bell for the start of lessons is about to go. Or, if you prefer, we'll go to the Head and I'll ask if I can take you home because you're not feeling well.'

'No, I'll come back to class,' Carl said.

The door opened and he came very hesitantly out, looking left and right like a burglar. He had a frightened look on his face, and Clive noticed for the first time how much thinner he'd got recently.

Clive took him by the arm and said, 'Look, I'm going to help you get rid of this vulture. I mean it. I've been doing a lot of thinking about it and after school we'll have a serious talk, OK?'

Carl nodded, but he'd have nodded at anything right then, Clive thought. Never mind, he'd get a pleasant surprise. He mightn't know, but Clive was serious. The vulture would know soon enough.

*

On the way out after school Clive didn't have to look up at the tree. He knew from Carl's relieved reaction, and sudden willingness to walk ahead, that the vulture wasn't on the branch. Clive was disappointed, as it would have been one way of knowing whether Carl was really seeing the vulture in places other than the roof-garden, or whether he was imagining it. Either way, it was real for Carl, and Clive had to get rid of it.

The bus came unusually quickly today, and for once the twins sat together. Carl's cronies didn't seem to mind. They'd obviously lost interest in him while he was in this mood, but they still didn't dare taunt him much about it. They mainly let him be.

'OK,' Clive said, immediately the bus moved off. 'It's because you're bad that the vulture hasn't melted. That's what I think.'

'Rubbish,' said Carl. 'That's impossible.'

'Well, look at how you built the vulture,' said Clive. 'You didn't make a snow-dove.'

'So?'

'And you have been really horrible recently. And the vulture's gone hard.'

'There can't be a connection,' said Carl loudly.

'It seems obvious to me,' Clive said, looking round.

'I'm not always bad,' Carl said. 'What about when I was upset? The vulture didn't go away then.'

'You won't get rid of it that quickly. And anyway, being upset is not the same as being good.'

'It's a load of nonsense, all this,' said Carl.

'Can you explain it any other way?' asked Clive.

'"Explain!" That's a laugh!'

'Suit yourself,' Clive said. 'Stew in it for all I care.'

Carl turned to the window in a sulk while Clive looked round to see if there were any empty seats in the bus. There was one, about halfway towards the back, beside a girl from his class. He hated sitting beside girls, but anything was better than sitting beside Carl. In any case, he needed to leave him to think about it. As the bus went into a straight bit of road Clive walked back and sat beside the girl amid the titters and whispers of her friends in the seat behind.

*

That evening Clive was happily seated at the kitchen table, painstakingly adding matches to the right shin of his match-man. His mother was out and his father was down at his desk writing letters. The door to the sitting-room was open and the gruff voice of Tom Waits was rhythmically growling from the speaker, and Clive was humming along.

Into this soothing scene came a gloomy, haunted-looking Carl.

'It's been down in the room again.'

'Oh, yeah?' said Clive, still concentrating on his matches.

'Please help me,' said Carl.

'You ready to listen?'

Out of the corner of his eye he saw Carl nod repeatedly.

'Good, because if I try to help you, I do it *my* way, and no other way, OK?'

He was looking straight at Carl now, who was nodding again.

'Any arguments and you're on your own.'

'Yes, yes,' said Carl.

'Go down to our room now, and I'll be down as soon as I finish this little bit and tidy up.'

Carl reluctantly backed out of the kitchen and went slowly down the stairs. Clive was smiling to himself, a big grin which he couldn't stop. He had never had such power over Carl before, and the funny thing was that this power had come out of badness – out of Carl's badness getting out of control.

The record was still playing as he went down the stairs and into the bedroom, closing the door behind him. First he took a blank page and a pen from a drawer in his desk, and a hard-covered book to lean on, and sat on the floor. He motioned to Carl to come down from his bunk and sit opposite him.

Carl was looking at the page and Clive preferred to say nothing yet, just to write slowly and dramatically in big letters at the top of the page: VULTURE PACT.

'What's "pact"?' asked Carl.

'You know, an agreement, a treaty.'

'What kind of a treaty?'

'Shush,' said Clive, and continued writing, every now and again stopping to think.

Between the Bein brothers on 21 March 1991. Clive will help his brother Carl get rid of the snow vulture if Carl promises to always do what Clive says.

Clive signed his name at the bottom, and handed the pen to Carl for him to do likewise. Carl hesitated.

'Hang on,' he said. 'This is a bit steep, isn't it? I mean, look at it – ". . . promises to always do what Clive says".'

'Don't you trust me?' asked Clive.

'How do I know what you're going to tell me to do? You could tell me to give all my toys to you.'

'Don't be stupid, I'm not like that. I'm only going to ask you to do things that will help you.'

'I don't like it at all,' said Carl.

'Well, you have no option, have you? It's sign it or no help, got it?'

'What kind of things are you going to make me do? You still haven't said.'

'I'm not sure yet. I'm keeping my options open.'

'You haven't a clue,' Carl said, 'and you want me to sign this?'

Clive blushed a bit and concentrated his thoughts. He wished he'd taken time to prepare his pact. Maybe he should have put Carl off till tomorrow. He could still do that.

Carl had been doing a bit of thinking himself, and was looking much less worried. He even had the beginnings of a smirk on his face.

'I'll sign it,' he said. 'It doesn't mean anything. Treaties are made to be broken.'

'You will not!' Clive said angrily. 'You only sign if

you mean it. Seems to me you're not serious about getting rid of the vulture. You still don't believe that it's because you're bad it won't go away. I'm wasting my time here.'

A frightened look came over Carl's face again.

'No, don't go. I need you to help me.'

'Well, do as I say then.'

At the same time Clive knew Carl's objections were justified, and the pact he'd drawn up was too vague. He tore the page in two, much to Carl's surprise.

'I'll draw up a better pact,' Clive said, 'and we can sign it tomorrow.'

'OK,' Carl said, relieved.

'But remember, it's serious. That's your only chance,' Clive said. He went to the bathroom to prepare himself for bed.

*

Although it was Saturday morning Clive was awake early and seated at his desk by the window. He was drafting a proper pact, a detailed one, one Carl would have no qualms about signing. Or so Clive hoped. It was in Carl's own interest, after all.

He chewed on his pen and looked out the window. It was the same old boring scene – trees, a wall, windows, a car park, and bins. Yet this window was where Carl claimed the vulture appeared. Clive didn't believe that. Still, as far as the vulture was concerned, he didn't know what to believe.

Carl hadn't woken yet, which was hardly surprising as he'd taken ages to get to sleep the previous night. He'd kept Clive awake too, with his repeated sitting up and shouting out, convinced that the vulture was in the room. He'd kept their parents awake as well, which was always a bad idea. The surprise was that Clive was up already, and hard at work. He had a mission, however, and couldn't rest until it was achieved. He had to get rid of the vulture.

The thought of the thing in the roof-garden gave him an idea. He rummaged in a drawer till he found his polaroid camera, his birthday present from his German gran last year. Then he quickly got dressed and ran up the stairs.

No one was up. The clock on the video showed 8.05, as he crossed the living-room and headed for the roof-garden. It occurred to him that, for all their obsession with it, neither he nor Carl had been up to see the vulture for days. Maybe . . . no, there it was, same as ever, a hunk of white malevolence. They wouldn't get rid of it that easily.

Clive tried to blank out the memory of the hammer bouncing off the vulture. He told himself it was a funny type of garden gnome, nothing else, but despite this he felt a little bit frightened being out there alone with it. He kept a foot in the door and raised the camera.

As he clicked the first time, he wondered if anything would show up on the photograph. Maybe, as with vampires throwing no reflections, snow vultures in their transformed state couldn't be photographed. When the print came out, however, it had the vulture clearly on it. Clive took a second photograph, and gratefully shut the roof garden door behind him.

Back at his desk he rummaged again till he found his badge-making equipment. He still had a few empty badges, and he cut up one of the photographs till it fitted, and he had a vulture badge. This would be an essential part of his treatment.

He was enjoying this very much. It made him feel good, so good he felt a bit guilty because Carl was so miserable. Still, it was all for Carl's good. He, Clive, was some kind of cross between a doctor and an exorcist, a modern, urban witch-doctor. And he was doing it all by himself.

Of course, he might not succeed, but he felt sure he would. He was the best chance Carl had, anyway. There was no way Carl could help himself, and no one else knew about it.

Carl woke as Clive bluetacked the second vulture photograph to the wall, high up near the ceiling.

'What are you doing?' Carl said, sitting up and backing towards the wall. 'Are you crazy? I thought you were trying to help me!'

'I *am* helping you,' Clive said. 'This is part of the treatment.'

'Some treatment! I'm not having it. I'm getting out to rip that photograph down.'

'Listen, stupid, I know what I'm doing. If you want help you'll play along. That photograph stays there. Ever heard of inoculation, like with a tetanus injection? Well, think of this as something similar.'

He wrote a little more at his desk and turned to Carl. 'Do you want to hear the new pact I've drawn up?'

'Suppose so,' said Carl.

'OK, here it is:

VULTURE PACT between Clive and Carl Bein on 22 March 1991 to get rid of the snow vulture. Carl Bein promises to be good, and Clive, his brother, will tell him the kind of things to do. Like being nice to people, not nasty. Carl will wear the vulture badge when he's out of the house, and will let the vulture photo stay on the bedroom wall. If he does all this Clive Bein promises the vulture will be gone by 22 September 1991.

There, you can't argue with that, can you?'

'There's lots I can argue with,' said Carl. 'We can start with the badge. Are you some kind of sadist, or what?'

'Look, I spoke to you about the photograph. The badge is the same thing for outside the house. Or, if you prefer, think of it as your guardian angel.'

'Very funny!' said Carl. 'And what about this "being nice to people"? Are you trying to turn me into some kind of goody-goody, or something, sitting at the front of the church, visiting the sick, that kind of thing?'

'Don't worry, Carl, I know you. I won't make you do corny things. That would be too boring altogether. I just want you to stop being nasty, start thinking of others. The first thing can be helping me with my match-man – *I'll* tell you what to do.'

'Hey, I don't want to work on your stupid match-man. I'm not your slave!'

'Carl, the vulture . . .'

Carl scowled and picked up the paper the pact was written on.

'This September date,' he said, 'it's six months

away. Do I have to put up with the vulture till then?'

'I don't know how long it will take to get rid of the vulture. I'd hope it would be quicker, much quicker. Don't worry about the date. You always have to put some date on a treaty.'

'I'm still not sure about it all,' said Carl.

'Sign it,' said Clive. 'It's for your own good. If you want the vulture gone badly enough you've nothing to lose.'

'That's what they say with all treaties,' muttered Carl. But he took the pen and signed the paper anyway.

Clive did likewise, saying as he did, 'Remember, if you break this treaty it's got its own punishment. The vulture will get you.'

Carl grimaced as he took the vulture badge from Clive and buried it in his pocket.

'All this had better work,' he said, 'or you won't see Christmas.'

*

Clive was astonished at how Carl threw himself into his 'treatment'. For the first week or so he supervised every move Carl made, went with him everywhere, set him tasks to do. Clive's match-man was the first to benefit from the change in Carl. Whereas the match-man had to be hidden from him before, Carl was now working away carefully at the right leg, taking directions from Clive and following the example of the completed left leg which stood on the table in front of him. Clive noticed, with pleasure, that the right leg was practically complete now too, and he had no criticisms whatsoever of Carl's workmanship. He felt especially pleased that the match-man was on the go again, as he'd more or less abandoned it recently. What was good, too, was the fact that he and Carl were working harmoniously together. It was a long time since that had happened. And Clive even thought that Carl was enjoying the work.

Clive himself was forging ahead with the upper part of the torso. He had decided to leave the arms for Carl, and he hoped he'd made the right decision. Still, if anything went wrong it could always be re-made. The one problem with the two of them working together was that they kept running out of matches. A test Clive put Carl through was to go round ringing all the neighbours' doorbells, asking if they'd keep their spent matches for him. He was extremely reluctant but Clive persuaded him, aided by the odd look in the direction of the roof-garden.

Their parents couldn't get over what they were seeing. They kept commenting on it, reacting in an exaggerated fashion.

'Are there three moons in the sky tonight, Carl?' asked their mother.

'When are you going off to become a monk?' was another remark.

'What kind of medicine have you been prescribed?'

Clive thought it quickly became tedious, and when the obvious one came – from their father, of course – 'Clive, why are there two of you, and where's Carl?', he said as much, and sent his father out of the kitchen in a mood.

It was dangerous, as well, what they were doing.

Weren't they pleased Carl's behaviour had improved? It must have been a great worry to them in the last while, with bad reports at school, not to mention his antics at home. Now they seemed to be provoking a bad reaction from him.

Still, they shouldn't be blamed. They didn't know what was going on. They obviously didn't believe Carl was any different, they merely thought he was taking a few days off from his normal behaviour. Maybe they were right. The leopard and its spots, and all that. Clive hoped, for Carl's sake, this wasn't so.

They'd given him an idea, however. He really had to test Carl. So one evening, when they were getting changed in their bedroom after school, Clive said in a matter-of-fact tone, 'You're a creep, Carl. And a sly one too. Here you are, pretending to be good, while all the time you're making a joke of it. It's typical of you.'

'What are you on about?'

'Come on, listen to yourself. Don't think I don't know. You can't change. You're bad through and through.'

'Hey, shut up! What are you saying all this for?'

'What are you saying all this for?' Clive mimicked. 'You're really brill this time, Carl. You've hidden your badness really well. No one who met you now for the first time would know. That makes you twice as bad.'

'SHUT UP! You know I'm really trying.'

'What should I call you now? Carl isn't bad enough. How about Beelzebub, Beelzy for short? Do you like that, Beelzy? Your vulture is waiting for your orders on the roof-garden.'

Carl clenched his fingers and took a step towards Clive.

'Go on, hit me, creep,' said Clive. 'Do it, do what you really want to.'

Carl hesitated, then turned and went out the door, banging it hard behind him. Clive looked up at the photograph at the top of the wall, among the pop stars, and pointed a forefinger at it and held it there.

*

Clive never let up. He kept Carl going at home – washing dishes, sweeping the kitchen floor, making his bed, hoovering, taking the rubbish out, bringing bottles to the bottle-bank. It became almost a game for Clive, but he was careful about this, afraid that it might jeopardize the chances of getting rid of the vulture if he didn't take the whole thing seriously. He once sent a very reluctant Carl up to weed the roof-garden, for even though the herbs and flowers hadn't grown, the weeds had flourished.

The most important part of the treatment, as Clive saw it, was not the helpful things Carl was doing, but how he had stopped being nasty to people. This was especially evident at school, where Clive spared Carl the need to be helpful. Tidying the teacher's desk would only draw embarrassment and scorn on Carl. That would do no good to anyone. But Carl didn't get in fights any longer, and stopped being a ringleader. Clive let him stand up for himself, however. That wasn't being bad. It was only keeping his self-respect.

He wore the vulture badge at all times at school, and it proved to be very popular. Kids kept asking him where he'd got it, much to Clive's amusement.

Carl handled it well, keeping the source a mystery. Clive was glad it was popular, as it made it easier for Carl to wear it, and so helped the treatment along.

Carl's performance in class improved as well, and this, together with better reports on his behaviour from his teacher and the Head, pleased his parents as much as it surprised them. They were beginning to believe that Carl had genuinely improved now, even if they were still wary. Who could blame them, after living with Carl for eleven years?

Clive had to fight against a growing boredom with Carl, and the treatment he had organized for him. He took to making half-serious demands. Once he made Carl offer to escort an elderly lady across a zebra crossing. The old lady thought he was a mugger and swiped at him with her umbrella.

Clive made them both sit on their bedroom floor, every now and then, for five minutes at a time and stare at the vulture photograph, as if trying to stare it out. He had to be careful their parents were occupied, as he'd have some explaining to do if they should walk in. All in all, he was pleased with Carl's progress. He hardly ever showed fear of the vulture now, or claimed to see it in their room or at school. Clive began to think his photograph and badge treatment was inspired.

But would it get rid of the vulture? For weeks now, Carl had pleaded for Clive to accompany him to the roof-garden, but Clive had refused.

'Don't rush things,' he'd said. 'The treatment will take time.'

Now, however, he felt they could go up there. He

waited till a Saturday morning when their parents were at the supermarket. He and Carl went up the stairs together, slowly, with Clive leading the way. Clive couldn't think of anything to say when he saw the accursed vulture still out there. He waited till Carl joined him on the top landing, and banged the glass door with his fist. Clive just stood there, demoralized.

Wait a minute, though, it was surely smaller and thinner! Weren't the eyes sticking out more from the head? Excitedly, he said this to Carl, asking him if he had the vulture badge with him. Carl dug it out of his pocket, and together they looked at it. Yes, there was no doubt, the vulture in the photograph looked bigger and stronger!

They couldn't get the door open quickly enough, though they still approached the vulture gingerly. Clive was marginally the more daring. He reached his right thumb out and pressed it hard against the vulture's head. It left a clear mark, although the texture wasn't as soft as snow! Heartened by this, Carl grabbed a brick and went to clobber the vulture but Clive stopped him.

'Don't do that,' he said. 'You'll wreck the treatment. And the treatment's working. The vulture's vanishing at its own speed. Provided you keep to the rules.'

Carl dropped the brick, reluctantly, and they both went in from the roof-garden, in better spirits than they had been for months.

*

It wasn't just that the good deeds stopped abruptly. Clive had expected them to run down. Hoovering and washing dishes wasn't Carl's style, and Clive hadn't intended insisting on them for much longer. It was that Carl's whole attitude reverted to what it had been before.

Well, not quite. He wasn't being horrible to Clive, beyond barking at him from time to time, and keeping his distance. And he didn't damage the match-man – he even, despite his grumpiness, helped build it occasionally. He was obviously grateful to Clive for the help he'd given him.

To his parents, however, he was as nasty as before. Disobedience, insolence, talking back were the order of the day. Even a walloping from his dad for throwing away the mail – including a sizeable cheque – even this didn't deter him. At school he was worse. It was as if he'd stored up all the little revenges he hadn't allowed himself to indulge in before. His most notorious act, that shocked his parents, not to mention the teachers, was what Carl himself proudly called his 'wet ambush'. During a lunch-hour he'd gone into the boys' toilets, turned all the taps on full and banged them with a stone till they were jammed. Soon there were several inches of water on the floor. He then ran out into the playground and whispered to all his old cronies in turn that there was a fight in the boys' toilet. Of course, they all ran in there, not stopping when they met the water, thinking, no doubt, it was connected with the fight. Carl locked them in by tying the doors securely together with a rope, and headed off down the wet corridor, chuckling. Even the severe punishment he got later didn't spoil his enjoyment.

But the vulture did! Carl had been working up to taking on the vulture. Even though he knew it was soft, he still couldn't bring himself to handle it. His mother had given him an idea, however. In her effort to coax the plants into growth – and there were now tiny green shoots showing in the pots – she had a hose permanently on the roof-garden, one end of which she'd bring in the kitchen window and attach to the tap. On a bright Sunday morning Carl offered to water the plants. To Clive's surprise, Carl was allowed to do this. Even Clive took too long to realize what Carl was up to. By the time he got up there, Carl was pointing the hose at the vulture and directing the full flow of water on it.

'No!' Clive shouted, knocking the hose away, till water went all over the roof-garden. It was too late. When Clive pressed the vulture as before, he found it as hard as stone. And it had filled out to its previous bulk. And there on its head was Clive's thumb-mark, showing how soft it had been, how much progress had been made before Carl ruined it.

*

Clive let Carl know exactly what he thought of him. Over and over again he told him, adding that Carl deserved the vulture, and he'd better get used to having it around, and to seeing it wherever he went, because he, Clive, was finished with it.

'Why don't you bring it down to the bedroom?' he said, sarcastically. 'It can have my bunk, if you like.

I'll sleep in the hammock on the roof-garden. We could lock you in, so you wouldn't be disturbed.'

Carl didn't react much to comments like these. A chucked shoe that was hardly meant to hit Clive was the worst. Usually it was a scowl, a muttered 'shut up', or a sullen silence. Clive soon grew tired of his own scolding, and threw himself into the building of his match-man like he'd never done before. Carl could stew in his situation, for all Clive cared.

Well, that wasn't true. What had really annoyed Clive was that they'd been so close to beating the vulture, and that he, Clive, had engineered it. He'd been like a football manager whose team had disobeyed his instructions during a match, and lost it after being ahead. Still, he realized there was no point in thinking this way. Carl's mad act couldn't be undone. Best to try and forget about it.

Between school and his match-man, not to mention reading and the odd TV programme, he did forget. He set himself a goal of having the match-man finished before the end of the summer term, so he could take it in to school and show it off. Maybe even plead with his parents for a party to celebrate its completion. The end of the summer term seemed a long way off, but progress had slowed a bit since Clive had started on the match-man's body. Not only was it bigger here, and therefore harder than a leg to keep together, but when he did succeed the result was so flimsy the slightest touch could break it up. The width was the problem. He did a lot of thinking about this. First he wondered if some kind of skeleton, made with thin strips of wood, was necessary. Then he experimented a little with double layers of matches, one inside the other. He finally opted for a compromise of sorts – reinforcing the inside of both front and back (he would do them separately, and glue them together at the end) with extra matches where they were most needed. It would still be fairly flimsy, but then he would never be standing the match-man up and kicking footballs at it.

There were problems, too, with the design. Sketches, then several false starts were needed before Clive was satisfied he could go ahead. He found himself looking at the legs that had come so easily, and wondering if he shouldn't make them over again, but he had enough hard work as it stood. Maybe the end of the autumn term would have been a more realistic goal. Maybe he'd never finish.

These new problems and negative moods were getting him down. He found himself missing Carl's help. Even if Carl didn't do much, his presence at the kitchen table on match-man-building occasions provided moral support. But Carl never came near him now. Clive presumed he spent most of his time down in the bedroom. Whenever Clive saw him, he had that old, anxious, depressed look mixed with a new one that was presumably guilt or remorse. He probably wanted to ask Clive to help him, as before, but didn't dare. And all because of the vulture.

Clive wondered if the vulture's powers went further than he'd previously imagined. Before, it had just been Carl who'd been affected. Could the vulture be responsible for the problems with the match-man and Clive's negative moods?

This was a bit far-fetched, he realized, but nothing was impossible. Still, now that the vulture was entering his thinking again, as a distraction, he realized he had to work again towards getting rid of it. He had to reactivate the pact. He glanced at the match-man, saying, 'I'm doing this for you, mate.' Then he headed off downstairs to find Carl.

*

Later he realized that he'd only needed the slightest excuse to get back to the pact. It had become a matter of pride to him to get rid of the vulture. As he'd expected, Carl had only been waiting for Clive to say something. He admitted he'd acted very stupidly. He promised he'd never do anything like that again. He'd been too eager, he said. He'd agree to any demands Clive would make, anything at all, provided it got rid of the vulture.

When Clive quizzed him he admitted that, yes, the vulture had been in the room again, several times, and in school too – even once in the classroom.

'It's very strange no one else saw it,' said Clive.

'It was during break, no one else was in the classroom.'

'Very convenient.'

Carl repeated his promises to be good from now on, and not to make the same mistake as before. He said he understood now how it was connected to his badness. Clive said he hoped so. He said he hoped a lesson had been learnt, but, knowing Carl, he doubted it.

'The only way we'll get rid of that vulture is my

way. Force won't work, you've found that out. The vulture can stand anything. If someone dropped a nuclear bomb on the roof-garden, right this minute, London would be flattened, we'd be history, but the vulture would be still here in the ruins – a bit dirty maybe, but that's all.'

Carl nodded, as if he really shared this belief.

'So we just carry on as before?' he said. 'Just as we agreed in the pact?'

'Yes, just as before. The same boring routine. With one or two extras thrown in, one or two surprises,' said Clive.

'What kind of surprises? Whose surprises?'

'Oh, for you, for the vulture.'

'For the *vulture*?'

'Yes, I thought it was time we started spending more time up there with it on the roof-garden.'

Clive noticed that Carl grimaced, but remembered his promise and said nothing.

'If you say you keep seeing it here in the bedroom or in school, you might as well see it where it lives. Visit it, like you would a friend. Save the vulture some trouble.'

He chuckled but Carl didn't see the funny side, just stared at Clive and said nothing. Clive continued. 'You can start by washing the vulture, *gently* washing it, not like last time. Get a sponge, and a basin of hot, soapy water. This London air is so dirty. Think of how dirty you'd get, stuck outside all the time. And the vulture is white.'

Carl looked at Clive in complete disbelief. He was serious about this! Carl opened his mouth to say something but Clive butted in.

'No arguments, that's the agreement, remember? We do this my way. And while you're at it, I think it would be a good idea to apologize to the vulture for what you did. In fact, I want to see you talking more to the vulture in future. You used to, remember, in the old days when you liked it.'

'I can't apologize to that thing,' Carl said, 'I hate it.'

'Well, who's to say you have to show it,' said Clive. 'It's time we were a bit sly about all this. This vulture won't be beaten easily. But we've done enough talking. Get that sponge and basin of soapy water, and give the vulture a surprise. I'll come up with you to make sure you do it properly. And maybe to say a few words to the vulture myself.'

*

If that vulture really had a mind, it certainly got a shock during the next few weeks. Clive saw to that. Not only was it washed once a week, till it was the cleanest garden object (or creature) in London, but it was frequently engaged in three-way conversation. Well, Clive would speak to Carl in the vulture's presence, and would frequently address the vulture or speak about it, but the vulture would never, of course, reply. Still, it was made part of things. It was introduced to music, as well, in that Clive took the transistor up to the roof-garden and played whatever pop music came on.

A regular photograph was taken, too, although Carl was dead against this. He didn't want to touch the vulture, let alone stand there with his arm around it, and a fake grin on his face. Clive insisted, however, saying it was part of the treatment. He took this photograph once a week, and stuck some up on the bedroom wall beside the solo photograph of the vulture and the pop stars. One he made into another badge for Carl to wear. He suggested that Carl take photographs himself, to sell to his friends and make some money out of the vulture.

It would be wrong to give the impression that the boys were untroubled by the vulture in those weeks. Carl was nervous at all times on the roof-garden, and would never go there alone. He never mentioned seeing the vulture elsewhere any more but that didn't mean he didn't. He had put himself in Clive's hands.

Even Clive was a lot more troubled than he let on, and he spent very little time alone up there. For all their efforts at pretending otherwise, there was still a bad aura attending the vulture. They couldn't stay up there long without becoming gloomy, and chilly, and argumentative. Clive spoke to Carl about this and they both agreed not to be provoked.

It was easy to get gloomy and think it was all a waste of time, with the vulture still dominating the roof-garden. What kept Clive going, though, was the memory of how it had weakened before. If it happened once it must happen again – and this time their tactics were even more organized. They still kept up the old ones, as well. Carl had cut out nastiness altogether (although, as usual, Clive wondered how long this could last) and was trying to be reasonably pleasant to people. He had resumed his helpfulness around the house, and his good efforts at school. Neither his parents nor his teachers, however, had forgotten his last bad outburst.

Still, they couldn't keep fighting indefinitely without some sign they were winning. Seeing the first sign became an obsession for both of them, but for Clive more than for Carl. He mightn't be as bothered by the vulture as Carl was, but he was more professionally involved. Every time he came up to the roof-garden he stared at the vulture for signs of change, but the vulture looked as firm and as filled-out as ever. He took to examining the weekly photographs under a magnifying glass, and lining one up against the other to look for any shrinkage, but even this brought no results. When Carl ridiculed this behaviour Clive retorted that direct comparison of photographs taken at different times was more likely to show changes; that tiny, gradual changes would not be noticed by visiting the vulture regularly. He took Carl upstairs to the living-room and got down the latest photograph album from its shelf, and in a whisper pointed out how their dad had put on weight in the past year, yet you wouldn't realize it, seeing him every day.

Just before the Easter break the first sign came. Clive excitedly looked up, with the magnifying glass in his hand, and shouted, 'It's shrinking! Come and see.'

Carl gave an anxious glance at the open window, knowing how clearly noise from downstairs could be heard on the roof-garden, but he still hurried over. At first, he couldn't see what Clive was talking about, but when Clive started moving the point of a pen (grown monstrous under the glass) around, like a measuring device, he thought he did.

They hurried up to the roof-garden to scrutinize the vulture directly. Sure enough, it showed! It was a slimmer vulture they were staring at. Carl said it was easier to see the change in the vulture itself – so much for Clive's comparison of photographs.

'Easy for you to say that now,' said Clive. 'Where did we notice the change first, tell me that?'

They didn't really feel like arguing, however. What they felt like doing was having a party on the roof-garden, taking up the transistor with drinks and biscuits, and dancing noisily around the vulture. They both knew that would be provocative, so they made do with a shared can of coke and a packet of cheese and onion crisps (bought with the remains of Carl's pocket money) in the bedroom. They each raised the coke-can to the photograph of the vulture and drank to its health, though of course they meant its ill-health.

*

Maybe that celebration was premature, as the vulture took a long time to go. It was worse than watching a hunger-striker, Clive thought one day on the roof-garden, worse because you *wanted* it to fade away. There were times when he wondered if he'd been mistaken in thinking the vulture had lost weight. A comparison of the photographs through a magnifying glass, however, always put his mind at rest. It *was* shrinking. Clive wished it would do so quicker.

He never let up on the treatment, needless to say.

Carl had been a model child for the past month. Whining about how long the vulture was taking to go was the worst Clive had to put up with. Their parents had come to accept the changed Carl, which Clive thought was a bit rash of them. (He still wasn't convinced, though Carl's fear of the vulture was reassuring.) They even took the boys out to a Greek restaurant, Carl's favourite, to celebrate. Clive didn't mind. He liked restaurants, and besides, the change was all his doing.

He was the one who did the naughtiest thing (though not in Carl's league) during that period. It happened on the roof-garden, of all places. That could have been dangerous, Clive knew, but he allowed it because it wasn't intended against the vulture (though the vulture was slightly affected). Besides, it was too good an opportunity to miss. His mother was sunbathing ridiculously early in the year. (Clive thought sunbathing was a ridiculous activity at any time, dangerous too.) She was lying on a blanket on the floor. Clive was up there watering the plants with the hose when he noticed she'd dropped off to sleep. He spoke to her softly to check, but she made no response. Next thing he knew, he'd grabbed a red towel from the washing line and blocked the drain with it. He then left the hose on the floor, with the water still gushing out of it, and went inside. Carl got the blame, of course, when their mother woke up, soaking. His repeated denials were waved away. It was too similar to his 'wet ambush' to be denied. Clive let his parents believe it was Carl. He thought it was good to have flashes of the old Carl on show, and it was better that he provided them, not Carl. The vulture preferred it that way.

Later he told an irate Carl that he hadn't intended to flood the roof-garden, that the vulture had made him do it. There may have been some truth in that. In any case, it didn't placate Carl, and Clive had no excuse for not admitting that he'd done it. Pact or no pact, Carl came very close to beating Clive up.

Shortly after this, Carl became impatient with the vulture. He took to going up to the roof-garden and glaring at the now pathetically frail creature.

'Why don't you go away,' he shouted.

Whenever he washed it (which Clive still made him do), he rubbed it so hard he left marks on it. Clive took him aside one day and warned him about this, reminding him about what had happened before. Carl's most bizarre antic was to set seven cloves of garlic in small flowerpots which he'd begged off his mother, and which he left near the vulture.

'You're getting confused,' Clive said to him, 'between vampires and vultures.'

'They're all the same,' Carl said. 'They're all evil.'

'You should know,' said Clive, leaving Carl to it.

To distract Carl, and himself, from the vulture, Clive got the match-man going again in a big way. It was irritating for him, this stopping and starting, but as is so often the case, he found that when he went back to it, the problems seemed smaller. He discovered he could build the body fairly easily, unlike before, when he'd doubted every move. Not for the first time he found himself looking up at the ceiling, above which sat the fading vulture, and wondering whether certain powers were on the wane.

While Clive was on the body, Carl made wonderful arms, with the most perfect hands. They were bunched in fists, and clearly recognizable as such. Clive didn't like to admit it, but he had a suspicion that Carl was better at this than he was. There was no justice in the world.

*

Their mother had a surprise for them at the summer half-term. She had rented a cottage in Cornwall, and they were going there for a week. Their father was taking a week off work. The boys heard about this on Friday afternoon, after school. They were to leave at 4 the next morning.

Even with such short notice they were excited. It was ages since they'd been on a holiday. And what a good time to go away, too, with this painful wait for the vulture to disappear. Carl whispered to Clive after dinner that the vulture would follow them, and recover its health in the process. Clive told him this wouldn't happen, although he was less than sure. Because of this, before bed (because he knew they wouldn't have time in the morning) he asked Carl to come with him to the roof-garden. They stood in front of the vulture which looked more like a scrawny chicken now, and was barely half a metre high.

'Vulture,' said Clive, almost solemnly, 'we're going away for a week. We've come to say goodbye.'

He elbowed Carl in the side.

'Goodbye,' spluttered Carl. He could manage no

more. The vulture's black eyes made no sign it understood.

'What did you make me do that for?' Carl said, when they got down to the bedroom. 'It was stupid. I felt a wally.'

'Who was afraid the vulture would follow him?' said Clive. 'I told you earlier we had to be sly to beat this vulture. We had to do things we mightn't think were necessary, or even sensible. The main thing is not to make the vulture mad – like you did before – and give it back its strength.'

Carl said nothing, just started throwing what clothes he'd need for the week into a rucksack, as his mother had ordered.

The cottage was very poky, but it was pleasant, and the village was lovely. Set at the top of an estuary, with thick woods on both banks of the river, it was the perfect place to spend a week. There were great walks through the woods (which, the twins' father told them, were the inspiration for the Wild Wood in *The Wind in the Willows*). Clive started collecting pocketfuls of tiny twigs to spruce up his match-man.

While they were down there, he and Carl worked together on the head, and Clive had a brainwave – to use the twigs from the woods to give the match-man dreadlocks. Working together, they took a surprisingly short time to finish the head, which was strikingly attractive, they thought. Even their mother agreed.

They did a lot of sightseeing, but the best part of the holiday for the boys was when, under their father's supervision, they went out in two canoes. Fully clad in lifejackets, they splashed around, almost trying to capsize. They raced to the arch of the bridge and back. Clive won the race twice, and Carl refused to do it a third time. Instead, he went off on his own downriver, till his father hollered for him to come back.

Carl got his revenge by beating Clive easily at pool in the pub next door, where children were allowed. He even beat their father once, though Clive said it was a fluke. Their father agreed. He hated losing at anything.

They sent loads of postcards. Clive joked they should send one to the vulture that they both missed very much. The only other time it was mentioned was the night before they went back, when Carl woke up from a nightmare in which the vulture was inside the flat. Clive sat up, switched the light on, and said:

'Did you see it? Is it here?'

'No,' said Carl.

'Go back to sleep, then. It doesn't matter.'

At Clive's suggestion, they passed the time on the long, boring motorway journey back by making the rest of the match-man's body. They unfolded newspapers on their knees – it was not as satisfactory as a table, but it would do. For some reason he didn't understand, Clive felt it was essential to have all the parts of the match-man finished by the time they got back. Then all they'd have to do was to glue the various bits together and there he'd be. 'Matman' was what Clive suggested he should be called.

Clive saw that Carl was getting nervous as they

neared London, and mistakes were creeping into his building. Clive took it from him, knowing that there was so little left he could easily do it himself. He whispered to Carl not to worry, that things would be alright. He was glad to notice, a little while later, that Carl had fallen asleep. He himself carried on with his match-man, glad he had something to do, and somewhere around Windsor, to his immense satisfaction, he glued the last match into place. Now he couldn't wait to get home to glue it all together. But accompanying the positive impatience was a negative one: would the vulture be gone?

*

'Well, we haven't been burgled,' said their father, as he carried the first of the luggage into the flat. While he went down to help their mother with the rest, the boys raced up the stairs, but halfway across the living-room Carl came to a stop.

'Come on,' said Clive. 'We may as well see what's there.'

'Or what's *not* there,' he whooped, as he got to the top of the stairs. He fumbled with the door-handle and ran out into a roof-garden with no trace of a vulture whatsoever.

'It's gone, it's gone,' he shouted, dancing around. Some old woman came out onto a balcony in one of the flats opposite, and peered at him. Clive didn't care. He carried on shouting and dancing.

Carl advanced into the roof-garden a lot more circumspectly. He stood where the vulture had been, and got down on his hunkers and felt all around, as if to see whether the vulture had merely become invisible, and was really still there. Then he walked slowly around the roof-garden, looking in every corner, even standing on the pile of bricks to look over the wall.

He still wasn't satisfied. Remembering his nightmare, he went inside and searched the flat from top to bottom. This irritated his dad who was relaxing with a cup of tea after the tiring journey. He didn't take too kindly to Carl looking behind his chair. Despite all this (to Clive, futile) searching, Carl found nothing. He went up to the roof-garden again, where Clive joined him.

'What's wrong with you?' Clive asked. 'Can't you see it's gone? Don't you want it gone, or something?'

'I can't believe it's gone, that's all.'

'Believe your eyes. It's not here. Full stop.'

Carl looked around him slowly again. 'That bay tree,' he said, 'it was never that big, was it? And doesn't it look like a vulture?'

Clive whistled in disbelief. 'And that cloud up there,' he said, 'looks like a monkey.'

He went in and left Carl alone.

He knew Carl was beginning to believe it when he came down to the living-room and banged the football so hard he came within inches of smashing the goldfish bowl into the wall. For that little trick his father sent him down to the bedroom.

Clive followed, to get rid of a little worry that had arisen.

'I hope that kick didn't mean you're back to your old tricks,' he said. 'The vulture might be gone but it can still come back. I think you know that yourself. Even if you move to the moon it'll get you. And I won't help you next time. So you'd better watch your behaviour, mate. And keep watching it.'

'For God's sake, Clive, I only kicked a ball.'

'OK, I'm just warning you. You're likely to forget.'

'How do you think it went?' asked Carl, in a quieter voice. 'Do you think it shrunk till it vanished into nothing? Or did it fly off somewhere?'

'I don't know. Shrunk, probably. It doesn't matter. It's gone. And it's only the first of June, four months early!'

'Come,' Clive continued, 'and we'll glue the bits of the match-man together. Make it complete. And tomorrow we'll varnish it black, and we'll put it in the roof-garden, exactly where the vulture stood.'

Carl nodded, with a bad-looking grin. 'And what'll we do then?' he said.

'I haven't a clue,' said Clive, surprised by the question.

'We could learn the guitar together,' said Carl, 'and later we could start a rock band, a really loud one. We could call ourselves *The Matchmen*.'

'Or *The Vultures*,' Clive said, '*The Snow Vultures*.'